"Ryan. Why did you come here tonight?"

Lounging against the end of her sofa, too large and too solid in her pretty front room, Ryan gave her a slow smile. "Would you believe me if I told you I just couldn't keep away?"

Meeting his gaze, she thought, *Yes*. Because she could see the truth there in his eyes.

He was as caught up in this connection between them as she was.

But then he shifted, sitting straighter, and carried on. "Truth be told...you were avoiding me, and I figured this was one place you couldn't just run away from. Not with Evie here."

"So you wanted to corner me? Why?"

"Because I have a proposition for you."

She suppressed a shiver at the word. "I'm not sure I like the sound of that."

"You will." His voice was firm, certain, and he inched a little closer as he spoke.

Gwen didn't move away as he continued.

Dear Reader,

If you're Welsh—or even mostly Welsh, like me—rugby is part of life. We're a small country, but rugby and singing are the two areas where we definitely punch above our weight—and I love both. So when I was assigned a rugby-loving Welsh editor, it was only a matter of time before we managed to sneak a rugby romance into the publishing schedule.

But this book isn't just about sport. It's about family, reputation, who we choose to be, forgiveness and, above all, second chances. Because when it comes to love, everyone deserves as many chances as it takes to find someone who loves them for the person they are—not the person others see them as.

Gwen and Ryan are both going to need to look deep, though—into themselves and each other—to find those true selves...but it'll definitely be worth it.

I hope you enjoy their story!

Love,

Sophie x

Second Chance for the Single Mom

Sophie Pembroke

Recycling programs
for this product may
not exist in your area.

ISBN-13: 978-1-335-55628-8

Second Chance for the Single Mom

Harlequin Enterprises ULC
22 Adelaide St. West, 40th Floor
Toronto, Ontario M5H 4E3, Canada
www.Harlequin.com

Printed in U.S.A.

Sophie Pembroke has been dreaming, reading and writing romance ever since she read her first Harlequin as part of her English literature degree at Lancaster University, so getting to write romantic fiction for a living really is a dream come true! Born in Abu Dhabi, Sophie grew up in Wales and now lives in a little Hertfordshire market town with her scientist husband, her incredibly imaginative and creative daughter and her adventurous, adorable little boy. In Sophie's world, happy *is* forever after, everything stops for tea and there's always time for one more page...

Books by Sophie Pembroke

Harlequin Romance

The Cattaneos' Christmas Miracles

CEO's Marriage Miracle

Wedding Island

Island Fling to Forever

Wedding of the Year

Slow Dance with the Best Man
Proposal for the Wedding Planner

Newborn Under the Christmas Tree
Road Trip with the Best Man
Carrying Her Millionaire's Baby
Pregnant on the Earl's Doorstep
Snowbound with the Heir

Visit the Author Profile page
at Harlequin.com for more titles.

For my brilliant, rugby-loving editor, Megan.

Praise for
Sophie Pembroke

CHAPTER ONE

GWEN PHILLIPS HELD her breath as around her the sound of the crowd built. Less than a minute left on the clock, and just a few too many metres between the Welsh team and the try line. But they had the ball in hand. If they could just break through the Irish defence, the game could be theirs.

Not just the game. The tournament. The championship.

Four points in it, that was all. One try, and it would all be over.

Then suddenly Williams broke free, side-stepped the defender lunging for him, and he was through and launching himself towards the ground, the ball just millimetres over the line, grasped tight in his arms.

They'd done it. They'd bloody well done it.

Around her, the stadium erupted with noise. Cheers and stamping and—of course—

singing. Joy and jubilation rang through the air, along with strains of 'Bread of Heaven'.

'Feed me till I want no more!' the crowd sang. And what more was there? For Welsh rugby, right now, this was the dream. And even Gwen, with her mixed feelings on the sport, couldn't help but grin, caught up in the moment.

Beside her, Joe grabbed her and lifted her in a tight hug, whooping in her ear, before turning to do the same to the stranger on his other side.

But as her feet touched the ground again, all Gwen could think was, *George would have loved this*. Her smile slipped away.

As if the thought had made the memory of her late husband real, Gwen looked down at the players on the pitch, slapping backs and hugging, and saw, impossibly, a familiar dark head atop memorable broad and muscled shoulders. He wasn't in the team strip but wearing one of the team hoodies instead. He hadn't been playing, he'd been sitting on the side, behind the subs benches, watching, she guessed. That was why she hadn't spotted him before.

George.

It couldn't be, of course. George had been dead for almost two years now. She'd seen his body, identified it after that terrible call from the police. Buried it. Cried with his parents. Explained to their daughter that Daddy wasn't coming home. That Daddy had been a hero, stopping a knife fight in a pub.

Told Evie anything but the truth, to keep her faith in and love for her father alive. To keep the memory of George one that his friends and family treasured.

They wouldn't, if they knew the truth.

Gwen shook her head to clear the memories, but she couldn't look away from the figure on the pitch.

Then the man looked up, a beaming smile across his face as he reached out to hug another player, and she realised, the truth hitting her hard in the chest.

Not George.

Ryan.

Ryan Phillips. Her brother-in-law, two years younger and with a reputation for being five times wilder than the respected, beloved captain of the Welsh team, George. The man who had actually introduced her to her husband, been best man at their wedding, a doting uncle to Evie for the first year, at least. And, until this moment, commonly understood to be living and playing rugby in France, ever since his shocking departure three years ago.

When did he come home? And why?

Would she find out? Or would his return remain as mysterious as his reasons for leaving in the first place?

'What is it?' Joe had apparently finished hugging every spectator he could reach—which, with his six-foot-plus ex-rugby player's build, was quite some way—and noticed her distraction. 'What's the matter?'

'Who do you see down there on the field?' she asked. 'The one in the grey hoodie, hugging Dewi right now?'

Joe leaned past her to get a good view, then swore. 'No wonder you're shaken up. For a moment there even I thought it was— Wait, is that *Ryan*?'

'Looks like it.' Gwen swallowed, and made herself look away. 'You didn't know he was back in the country either, then?' She'd hoped not; if he'd known and not told her, she'd have been properly miffed.

Joe shook his head. 'No idea. But if he's down there with the team, I'd place money he's planning on coming back to play.'

'Which means a new team, here in Wales.' Welsh rugby rules meant that, because he hadn't played enough games for the national team before he'd transferred to play club rugby in France, Ryan had been ineligible to play for Wales for nearly three years now. But if he'd transferred back to a Welsh club...

'They kept that bloody quiet,' Joe said. 'Well. I promised the boys I'd stop by the hotel later, stand them a pint. I'll find out what's going on for you.'

But the possibilities were already swirling around Gwen's brain.

George's death had been a tragedy, everyone agreed with that. His accident, six months before he'd died, had been a shocking loss to the world of rugby too. Cut off in his prime, so to speak. Even now, commentators still speculated on what the team might be if he hadn't been forced to give up the game so young—although maybe less so after this tournament.

That Ryan had left the country just two games before the one that had injured George had been a talking point too. Could George's little brother have protected him if he'd been playing there at his side, as normal? They'd always had a strange synchronicity on the pitch, an uncanny ability to know where the other was at all times. It had led to Ryan supporting George to try after try, either by passing him the ball at the critical moment, or distracting defenders and keeping them away.

No one had quite believed it when Ryan had declared he was leaving Wales. George least of all. Gwen remembered the yelling, the slammed doors as Ryan had walked out for the last time. And as she'd heard the names George had called his brother, she'd wondered, for the first time, if maybe Ryan hadn't got the right idea.

Maybe it was time to get out.

Everyone in Wales remembered George as a hero, especially his family. Well, everyone except Gwen, and Joe. But they weren't telling.

Evie knew her father was a hero, and that was what mattered most. Gwen would do anything to keep that illusion alive. The little girl had lost so much already, the last thing Gwen wanted was for her to have to face the truth about her father before she was old enough to understand it.

George had been a good man, and a hero of Welsh rugby, and that was how he should be remembered. Not as the man he'd become, especially after his accident.

It was bad enough that Gwen had to remember that man, rather than the loving, supportive one she'd married. People changed, she knew that. But legacies didn't.

And it was to that end that Gwen had set up the George Phillips Trust, helping those who'd suffered life-changing brain injuries, in sport or otherwise. George had always had a healthy life insurance policy, and the pay-out had meant that money was at least one thing Gwen didn't need to worry about. Building up the trust—fundraising, learning from experts, trying to educate the public—that felt worthwhile. Like she was making a difference.

It was the legacy she wished George had really left for her and for Evie. And since he couldn't, she would.

But the George Phillips Trust was one more charitable cause in a world full of those in need. Getting the attention she required to raise the money that was so desperately needed was almost impossible.

Unless she had a platform. A kind of celebrity that brought its own attention, wherever it went.

Already she could hear those in the stalls around her murmuring, wondering, as they noticed the new figure on the field—the way she had. Ryan Phillips was a name too— maybe not as big as his brother's, and perhaps fading a little in the collective memory before now, but still a name. And this unexpected return to his home country would be bound to raise his star a few notches.

Ryan had always been the tabloid favourite anyway. With their stunning looks, the Phillips brothers had been photogenic, they'd been friends with celebs, and they had been at the top of their game. And while George had settled down with her, had Evie, and given up the headline-inducing lifestyle, Ryan had done the opposite. It was a rare weekend that didn't yield a photo of him drunk with some teammates, falling out of cars, or with a soap star or pop singer hanging off his arm. His parents had despaired of him, of the embarrassment and shame he brought with every new headline.

'Why can't you be more like your brother?' his mother had used to ask, shoving the newspapers into the recycling bin.

Ryan had always just shrugged, smiled and gone his own way again.

He had been the wild-child brother to George's golden boy. That was just who they'd been.

But now…. Now that wild-child reputation could be good for something at last. People knew his name, liked his face. They'd pay attention to what he said.

Ryan could get her the publicity she needed to put the trust on the map. To cement George's legacy. To enable her to help others, so maybe they didn't have to go through what she had. What George had. What Evie had.

She just had to persuade him to help and not hinder the operation.

Which probably would have been easier if she'd spoken to him since the funeral. And if he hadn't fallen out with every other member of his family in such dramatic style the day they'd buried George.

But just because it might be hard it didn't mean it wasn't worth trying.

Straightening her shoulders, she turned to Joe. Two long years she'd been away from the rugby scene. But apparently it was time to head back in.

However scary that sounded.

'You're going to the team hotel?' she asked. 'Great. Then I'll go with you.'

'That was incredible, mate!' Ryan wrapped his arms around Dewi and smacked a kiss to the side of his head. 'The championship-winning try. I knew you had it in you!'

Back when Ryan had still played for Wales, his last season there in fact, Dewi had been the new boy on the team—barely nineteen and had hardly played for a club before, let alone his country. He'd been so wet behind the ears Ryan had taken him under his wing, just to make sure he survived all the training-camp pranks the rest of the team liked to pull.

And now he was the tournament-winning try-scorer.

Ryan ignored the part of his heart that ached at not being out there on that field today, the way it always did when Wales played, especially at home at the stadium in Cardiff.

Maybe, this time next year, he'd be out on the pitch with them. Sooner, he hoped.

He was ready for it, he knew that. It was why he'd decided to come back. Why he'd asked his agent to put feelers out for any offers from a Welsh club, however much of a drop in salary he had to take.

People thought he'd sold out to play in France for the money. They couldn't have been more wrong, but at least the cash meant he could do whatever he wanted now, regardless of the pay.

It had taken him three years, but he was ready to be back in Wales again, playing for his country.

Now he just had to persuade them to give him the chance.

'You coming back to the hotel?' Dewi asked. 'Celebrate with us?'

'Wouldn't miss it,' Ryan said, with an easy smile. They'd all be so far into their cups within half an hour they'd never notice his switch to non-alcoholic beer, rather than the pints of bitter he used to prefer. It wasn't the not drinking he minded, just the questions that always went with it. He didn't want to start explaining himself, or who he'd decided to be now, until he'd settled in a little more.

He wasn't the Ryan Phillips they all remembered, and that was a good thing, he hoped.

The hotel was nearby, so Ryan left the team showering and changing, doing interviews and signing daffodil hats and dragon banners. He'd head over, get changed, and meet them all in the bar.

But first there was one last person he needed to congratulate, still out in the stadium.

'That was one hell of a game, boss,' he said, as he caught up with Freddie Yates, the Welsh coach.

Freddie turned, his weathered face cracking into something that almost resembled a smile. 'Wasn't bad, was it?'

'That must make it, what? Your fourth

championship title?' It was Freddie's third in charge of the team, Ryan knew, but a little flattery never went amiss in situations like this.

'Third, as you well remember,' Freddie replied. 'Who knows? You play your cards right this season, you could be on the pitch for the fourth, next spring.'

'That's what I came back for,' Ryan said, with an easy shrug, even as the thrill of the possibility ran through him.

His words were true, even if it wasn't the full story. The lure of playing for his country had never gone away, despite his choice to forfeit it for a time. He knew that his teammates had never understood his decision—they knew he wasn't in it for the money, even if the rest of the country didn't. But that just made it more inexplicable for them. What could Ryan possibly get in France that he couldn't have here in Wales? And why would he give up on them, their team, his own brother, and playing together?

Ryan hadn't even bothered to try and explain. They couldn't ever understand. Because they'd never had the perfect George Phillips as an older brother.

When they'd been younger, he'd thought the two of them were their own team. Then as George had got older, stronger, better, all Ryan had wanted was to follow the trail he'd blazed. And he had. Same training regime, same youth team, same agent, same opportunities—although he'd been sure to work for a different position on the team, so he'd never be in direct competition with his big brother.

Even growing up, Ryan had known that George was the star, the one his mother had bragged about to anyone who would listen. But back then he'd believed that if he did the same, she'd feel the same way about him.

Except that had never happened. Even when he'd started playing professionally, got selected for the Welsh team for the first time... she had been more concerned with how many tries George had scored, or whether he'd get to be captain.

And Ryan had known, for sure, that he'd never live up to George's reputation. So he'd decided to stop even trying. He'd chosen instead to be the opposite of George's shining example.

The wild brother, the troublemaker. The disappointment.

At least his mother acknowledged his existence when she complained about him being photographed falling out of another taxi, drunk, with some soap star. And, really, why bother trying when he was never going to be enough for anyone?

Eventually, though, he'd had to admit that even that didn't fill the hole inside him. He'd stopped trying to be George, only to switch to playing the anti-George instead. His whole world had still centred around his golden-boy brother. The realisation, too late to change anything, he'd thought, had burned through him, and filled him with resentment.

Until one morning he'd woken up, hung-over and late for training, with a woman he hadn't even recognised in his bed, and something inside him had just said—

Enough.

He'd never be able to find his own path, decide who he really wanted to be, reach his full potential, while he was living in his brother's looming six-foot-four shadow. In Wales, he'd always be the younger, lesser Phillips brother. They couldn't see him any other way.

In France, they might let him play as himself. Live as himself.

He'd called his agent that evening and asked him to find him another team, on the Continent. And he'd taken the first offer he'd received.

It wasn't perfect, and it had cost him a lot— cost him his family in the end. If he'd seen that coming, he might have thought again. If he'd known that in just two games' time George would be injured. That in a year and a half he'd be dead...would he still have gone? Ryan didn't know.

But if he hadn't, then he wouldn't be the person he was now. And today's Ryan Phillips was a hell of a lot more comfortable in his own skin than he'd ever been before.

That was what had made him feel able to come home, at last.

This time, he'd woken up alone, in his house in France, well rested and early for training. He was in peak physical condition, playing the rugby of his life...but he'd known, suddenly, he was in the wrong place.

It was time. Time to put the past behind him. George's accident, his death, the awful row with his parents, Gwen...everything.

He wanted his family back. His country back. His future back.

And he intended to get them.

Playing rugby in Wales again was only the start. Playing *for* Wales would be a big step.

But rugby wasn't what had brought him home.

He'd come home for his family. To show them the man he'd been meant to be all along.

It was just that the rugby was the easier part to start with.

Freddie clapped a hand against his shoulder, still hard enough to smart even now, when it had to be thirty years since the coach had played a rugby match.

'You keep your nose clean, lad, and maybe you'll get out there sooner than I think.' There was a seriousness in Freddie's gaze that calmed Ryan's excitement at the words. 'It's time to put your past in the past, son.'

'That's the other thing I came back for.' Ryan held the older man's gaze, no hint of flippancy in his voice.

Freddie studied him for a moment, then nodded. 'Good.' Then he smiled; a real, honest, actual smile. Something Ryan was certain he'd never seen on the coach's face before. 'Very good.'

Ryan's chest felt lighter instantly. As if one small segment of the weight he'd been carrying around on his heart had lifted.

He was doing the right thing. He could come home. He could move on, past everything that had happened before. One person believed in him, and that made the world of difference, it seemed.

Put the past in the past.

For the first time in three years that actually felt possible.

He looked up, as another cheer went around the stadium, and he saw that the screens were replaying the moment Wales had won, in reactions from fans around the stadium this time, instead of what had happened on the pitch. Apparently one camera had managed to zoom in on the legendary Joe Evans—the Welsh scrum half who'd captained the team for years and had retired the season before Ryan had got called up to play for Wales. He'd been a friend of George's, though, when they'd played together.

He smiled at the sight of him on the screen, larger than life, arms raised in a cheer, mouth wide and yelling, jumping to his feet as the magic happened.

But his smile slipped away as her realised who was sitting next to him, fists against her mouth, watching as if she didn't believe it could be true.

Gwen.

The other reason he'd left Wales, although he'd never admitted that. Not even to himself, until he'd been hundreds of miles away, and a long way further down his path to understanding why he did the things he did.

His brother's wife. The one woman in the world he couldn't, shouldn't want.

And the only one he desperately did.

Back then, he'd assumed it was just another case of wanting what came so easily to George. He'd had the fame, the glory, the adoration of a nation, the willpower and self-control not to screw it all up, like Ryan tended to. His suspension after starting a brawl with the opposing team was still a low point in Ryan's personal and professional history. As was the red card in the World Cup quarter-finals, for that matter.

But being Wales's golden boy hadn't been enough for George. He'd had to marry the most perfect woman too. The ideal rugby player's wife—supportive, loving, beautiful, intelligent, and she genuinely loved the game. Any bloke would be a little envious, right?

And the worst part was that Ryan had met her first. *He'd* been the one who'd spotted her with her friends in the bar. The one who'd bought her a drink and tried to chat her up. The one who might have succeeded if he hadn't been lured away by the promise of shots with the guys, promising Gwen he'd be right back…

Of course, by the time he'd returned, George had already swooped in, his usual, charming self. More charming, more handsome, and definitely more sober than Ryan. Was it any surprise that George had been the one to get her number at the end of the night?

At the time, Ryan had rolled his eyes and moved on. It had only been once he'd got to know Gwen properly, spent time with her as family, that he'd realised how much more he'd given up that night.

Realised how much more she meant to him, as well as George.

He'd been right to leave, he'd never doubted that, even when the rest of the nation had.

But now he was back…he wondered if there was one piece of his past, of the person he'd been, that he'd never be able to put behind him, however hard he tried. A part that would always call to him, no matter where he went or what he did.

Gwen.

'Are you really sure you want to do this?' Joe asked, as he handed her the gin and tonic he'd ordered for her. 'I can find out what's going on. You don't have to be here.'

The security around the exclusive Cardiff hotel where the Welsh team was staying had been hefty, but Joe's famous face had got them in with no trouble. Now they were sitting in the fancy bar, waiting for the boys to show up in their suits and ties, all the mud washed away, even if the bruises remained.

Any minute now, Gwen told herself as she watched the door. Any minute now they'd all flood in.

'It will be nice to see them all again.' It wasn't really a lie; a lot of the guys on the team had played with George, and even the ones who hadn't had known him. She'd attended parties and team barbeques and awards ceremonies with plenty of them. They were the people she needed to keep in touch with, to help with the George Phillips Trust. This was good. It was work.

It was also a little bit terrifying.

When George had been injured, when he'd realised the damage to his arm and shoulder meant he'd never play again, he'd pulled away from all his old friends. For a time, they'd tried to visit, to see how he was doing. But Gwen had known he'd hate any of them to *really* know how he was—depressed, angry, reckless and irrational. At least, the old George would have. The new George hadn't seemed to care.

She'd cared. So she'd stage managed those visits as best as she could, keeping everything calm and relaxed, steering the conversation away from any of George's flash points, the topics that would send him into a rage without warning.

It had been exhausting.

But as the weeks had passed, the number of flash points had seemed to grow and grow, until they'd encompassed almost everything.

Joe had been there when she'd finally lost control of the situation, and George had blown up at her, at Evie for crying, even at Joe for being there at all. The raging, the yelling, the thrown mug crashed against the wall with tea dripping down the paintwork... Joe had seen it all.

He was the only one who knew the truth.

'It's not really him talking,' she'd tried to explain, after George had stormed out. *'It's the injury. It wasn't just his arm and shoulder he injured when he fell, you know. The blow to the head was the more worrying thing. Head injuries...they're funny beasts, his doctor says. And this was such a bad one. He can't... He just can't go back to the man he was before. His brain won't let him.'*

The man she'd married had been gentle, kind, however rough he'd been out on the pitch. And whatever problems they'd had in their marriage in the last months or year before his accident, he'd never been like *that* before. Then she'd been able to tell herself that it was the stress of the captaincy weighing on him, or being parent to a young child. That all marriages went through rough patches.

Now she didn't bother lying to herself. This was who he was.

She'd married George for better or for worse, in sickness and in health.

She just hadn't imagined that the sickness could make him a different person entirely.

Gwen shook away the memory. None of the boys on that pitch today knew what George had become, and she intended to keep it that way. To protect his memory. To them, she was still the sad widow who had lost the love of her life.

They didn't know he'd died the day that tackle had gone wrong, and the man she'd lived with for eighteen months after that had been someone else altogether.

Not even his own brother knew that.

Joe was giving her a sceptical look, like he knew exactly where her thoughts had gone. But then he straightened up, his attention diverted to the door. 'Here he is.'

Ryan hadn't been playing, of course, so had made it back before the rest of the team. But it seemed he'd still taken the opportunity to smarten up before the evening's festivities. Probably hoping to score with one of the many rugby groupies, knowing Ryan—unless he had his own minor celeb in tow, ready for the tabloid shots. Circulation figures for some of Britain's best-known gossip mags must have gone down since Ryan Phillips had stopped gracing their pages, she was sure.

His grey suit fitted him perfectly, as always, skimming over the heavy muscles she knew were underneath. She'd seen him play on the telly only once since he'd moved to his club in France—and that had been by accident, when trying to find English children's television for Evie in a French hotel room on holiday. He hadn't lost any form—or muscle—since his transfer, she'd seen enough to know that. If anything, reports had said he was playing better than ever.

Ryan's sharp blue eyes flashed as he glanced around the room, obviously looking for someone worth seeing and landing on Joe. With a smile, he began to cross the bar towards them. From where she was sitting, Gwen realised he probably couldn't see her, hidden in the shadow of the bulky ex-captain. But she knew the moment he spotted her. His stride faltered, just for a second, but it was enough.

She'd never really understood what had

driven Ryan away from his homeland, but she knew why he'd never come back. What had changed? Why was he here now? She knew she wouldn't rest until she understood. Despite everything, Ryan was family. And that mattered to her.

When she and George had first started dating, Ryan and his parents had been welcoming and friendly. When they'd married, she'd been accepted into the family as if she'd always been there. With her own parents dead, that had meant the world to her. And when Evie had come along, everyone had been thrilled. She'd teased Ryan about settling down one day too, and he'd laughed and said that they all had George for that. Everything had been perfect.

The fractures in their happy family unit had started before George's accident, though. They'd begun the day Ryan had announced he was signing with a French club and leaving Cardiff. No one had understood why, and he wouldn't or couldn't explain. Even George hadn't been able to get his reasoning out of him, although they'd argued until the small hours.

Gwen remembered curling up in bed alone, praying they wouldn't wake Evie. That George wouldn't disappear out again when they were done, the way he'd taken to doing over the last few months, never telling her where he was going.

Ryan had left, and two games later George had been injured. And the first thing his mother Meredith had said was, *'This wouldn't have happened if Ryan had been on that pitch to protect him.'*

She remembered being so taken aback at that. Gwen had always thought that big brothers were supposed to look after their younger siblings. But in the Phillips family it was different—even if it had never been said so starkly before. George was supposed to shine, and Ryan was needed to clear his path and keep him safe. The day he'd left, she remembered George yelling, 'But I need you on my flank! I don't trust anyone else there!'

Looking at him now as he crossed the bar, Gwen wondered if *that* was the real reason Ryan had left. Maybe he'd been sick of always playing back-up to his big brother.

But now he was the only Phillips brother left.

There had been a moment at the funeral—one she didn't think anyone else had seen. A moment when Ryan had leaned over the coffin, after everyone else had gone, and had said, so softly she'd strained to hear, 'I'm sorry. I should have been there on your flank.'

And from the stricken expression on his face when he looked at her now, Gwen knew instantly that, fairly or not, he still blamed himself for not being there to save George. Not on the pitch, and not in that Cardiff bar eighteen months later when George had been stabbed in a knife fight and had bled out before the paramedics even reached him.

'He was all on his own,' Meredith had sobbed into Gwen's shoulder at the hospital. *'Where were his friends? Where was his brother? My golden boy...'*

He hadn't been alone, Gwen knew. He'd been with another woman, for a start. One who'd sobbed and screamed dramatically— but had then disappeared when the police started to ask questions, apparently. But Meredith didn't need to know that. No one did.

'Joe.' Ryan reached the table and held out a hand. 'And Gwen. I saw you both on the big screen at the game, but I didn't expect to see you here.'

Gwen got to her feet and moved to hug her brother-in-law. 'We could say the same about you, you know. Do your mam and dad even know you're back in the country?'

Ryan returned the hug tentatively, as if

afraid he might break her. Or maybe just unsure of his welcome here.

He gave her a lopsided smile. 'I thought it would be a surprise.'

Not a *nice* surprise, she noted. Just a surprise. 'I imagine it will.'

'And you two.' Ryan motioned between Gwen and Joe. 'Are you two…?'

It took her a moment to realise what he was asking. Joe got it first, and laughed.

'I think my husband would disapprove,' he said lightly, although Gwen knew how much those words cost him. How he expected to be judged still, every time. 'But Ben has no interest in rugby. He's always grateful when Gwen takes me out, because it means he doesn't have to come.'

Ryan's smile was genuine, and Gwen felt something relax inside her. 'I didn't know you were married. Congratulations.'

'Thanks.' Joe's shoulders relaxed too, Gwen was glad to see. 'What are you drinking? I'll get the pints in.' He drained his own and waited for Ryan to answer.

'Ah, whatever's on draught, please, mate,' he said, after a long moment where Gwen almost expected him to say something else— although what, she had no idea. Ryan had never been one to turn down a pint.

She motioned to the spare seat at their table, and he took it as Joe ambled off towards the bar.

'So you here to congratulate the team?' Ryan asked. 'It was a great game, huh?'

'Amazing,' Gwen agreed. But she wasn't thinking about the game. She was thinking about the George Phillips Trust. About Evie, and the father she deserved to remember. This was her chance. So she took a deep breath and said, 'Actually… I saw you at the stadium and, well, when Joe said he was coming here I decided to come too. Because I wanted to talk to you.'

CHAPTER TWO

OKAY, HE HADN'T expected that. To be honest, he didn't really know what he'd expected. For her to ignore him perhaps? To walk out the moment she saw him? Or maybe just an awkward sort of reunion that would end as soon as they could both leave.

Ryan wasn't under any illusion that his return to Wales would be good news in all quarters. Quite apart from the fans and teammates who felt betrayed, he knew he had a long way to go to make up with his parents after the events of George's funeral. He'd expected a lot of apologising and begging to get any of his family to even speak with him. But if Gwen was willing—no, wanting—to talk to him, maybe things weren't all that hopeless after all.

When he'd seen Joe sitting there in the bar he hadn't imagined for a moment that Gwen would be there with him. Time was she would always have been there with George, but Ryan didn't think he'd seen Gwen out with the team since Evie was born. But then he'd turned towards their table and seen her—and suddenly all those old feelings had come flooding back. The ones he'd moved across the Channel to get away from.

God. Lusting after his brother's wife. He really was the lowest of the low—even if she was now technically his brother's widow. She hadn't been when he'd fallen for her. And now…even thinking about Gwen that way felt like he was *glad* that his brother was dead.

He wasn't. Whatever his nightmares told him sometimes.

'You wanted to talk to *me*?' he asked, just to check he'd heard her right. It wasn't the first time his imagination had told him she was saying something she wasn't. Luckily, he'd always been very clear on the reality of the situation, and he knew his brain was a lying creature.

She nodded. 'I've been working on a new project. One I was hoping you might be able to help me with.'

She needed help? His help?

A war was starting in Ryan's head. Part of him knew he do anything Gwen needed, anything she asked for. Another part knew that was probably the worst option available to him. He'd wanted to come home to Wales to be closer to his family, but now he was here he could already see perils that lay ahead on that path. Reconnecting with his family meant reconnecting with Gwen too. And that could be fine, as long as it was in a sisterly, see her on birthdays and holidays kind of relationship. One that centred around him being Uncle Ryan to Evie, perhaps.

Anything more…that was just asking for his own personal, miserable hell.

He'd forgotten. No, not forgotten. He'd thought he must be imagining it. Over the years away he'd convinced himself that the kind of connection he felt with Gwen couldn't be a strong as he remembered. He'd thought it must have faded over time. That she'd have changed, or he would have.

But here, now, he knew that nothing had changed.

In fact, nothing had changed since that first night he'd seen her across the bar and pushed his way through the crowd to meet her. Except now he wouldn't let anything tempt him away from her for a second, if he had that chance again. And certainly not a tray of shots with the boys.

'What project could need an aging rugby player?' he asked. 'And, actually, if that's what you need, I reckon Joe would be a much better bet.'

'If you don't want to help—' Gwen started, and Ryan instantly felt guilty. He knew how much it must have cost her to come here to this place, with all these memories, and ask him for his help. Gwen was a proud woman, and she wouldn't ask if it wasn't important.

'No! I didn't say that,' Ryan said. He shook his head, partly to support his point and partly to try and shake away all the wrong thoughts he had about the woman in front of him. 'What is it? What do you need? Is it Evie?' Horrible thoughts filled his head. What if it was Evie? What if while he'd been away, dealing with all his issues, Gwen had been needing him and unable to ask? He'd never forgive himself for that. For letting his family down again by not being where they needed him.

'No, no. It's nothing like that. Evie is fine.'

'I should have asked. I mean, I've been thinking about her. And you.' Was he giving too much away? Ryan couldn't tell. Suddenly it felt important that she know he hadn't just forgotten all about them and moved away, even if that was how it had seemed. 'How are you?'

'I'll be better if you agree to help me,' she said.

Her smile was too bright. Ryan watched her carefully she waited for his answer. There was something behind her eyes he didn't think he'd ever seen before. Darkness, almost. Darkness that certainly hadn't been there when he'd left.

But before he could question it, Joe returned from the bar with their drinks, plonking them on the table with a nod towards the door. 'Incoming,' he said.

Ryan looked up and saw the victorious team making their way into the bar, suited and booted and ready to drink. He grinned as Dewi headed straight for him, his blond hair still wet from the shower. He wasn't alone either. Even after so long away he still had plenty of mates on the team, ones who remembered exactly how good he was at celebrating—or commiserating when it came to it.

'Ryan! You ready for another pint yet?' Dewi clapped him on the shoulder.

'I haven't had a chance to start this one yet,' he pointed out. Across the table, the darkness behind Gwen's eyes had only grown. Joe had taken his seat beside her, sitting close, almost protectively. Shielding her from the crowd with his body.

All the same, Dewi spotted their companion and his eyes widened. 'Gwen! I didn't see you there. Were you at the game? Here, let me get you a drink. Guys! Look who's here!'

As the rest the boys headed over towards the table, drawn not just by the presence of Ryan and Joe but by the unexpected addition of Gwen Phillips in her role as tragic widow, Ryan watched Gwen shrink in on herself. He'd wondered if perhaps going to games with Joe and meeting up with the team afterwards was something she'd done more of while he'd been away. But he thought now this really was a one-off. She'd come here to see him, and now she had to face the entire Welsh rugby team.

Whatever she needed from him must be really important.

Ryan got his feet and, with an easy charm he'd almost forgotten he possessed, managed to steer the team towards the bar instead of Gwen. 'That was quite some match, guys. Only thing that could have made that victory better was if I'd been on the field with you. Now, how about I get the first round in to celebrate?'

Handing his credit card over to Dewi, Ryan left them placing their orders at the bar. Then, when he was sure that none of them were watching, he slipped back to the table, gave Joe a nod he knew the older man would understand, and took Gwen's arm.

'Come on,' he said. 'I think we need somewhere quieter for this conversation, don't you?'

Gwen glanced at Joe too, as if for approval, and then nodded.

The whole hotel was buzzing with fans, press and other hangers-on. Ryan kept his head down as he led Gwen towards the small hidden nook he'd found the night before. The table and two small bench seats were nicely hidden from the rest of the bar and the crowds.

Gwen's shoulders started to relax the moment she sat down, and Ryan could see the darkness behind her eyes starting to fade.

'Better?' he asked.

Gwen gave him a sheepish smile. 'I don't like crowds so much these days.'

'And that wasn't just any old crowd,' he joked. 'You haven't seen them much since…' Ryan trailed off, not wanting to have to say the words.

'No. Not since the funeral.'

She didn't have to say anything else. Ryan knew they both remembered the events of that day well enough without hashing them out all over again.

Time to change the subject. 'So? You wanted to talk to me about something?'

'Yes.' She straightened little in her seat, and suddenly Ryan was reminded of all the disciplinary panels he'd ever had to attend. At least this time he was fairly sure he hadn't actually done anything wrong. Well, not recently, anyway. 'Late last year, I decided to start a trust in George's memory. Evie and I… We had the insurance money, plus our savings, and the house. We were really lucky. But I know a lot of people who suffer the sort of life-changing injuries George did—the sort that mean giving up a job they love, or needing help at home and so on—wouldn't be so lucky. And I thought if we could help them maybe that would help me… I don't know. Find meaning in what happened, maybe.'

'That makes sense,' Ryan said. Although he didn't see what it had to do with him, or how he could possibly help. He hadn't even been there when George had got injured. Helping people was clearly not his strong point. 'What you want me to do?'

'I know you have been away a while, but you're still a name over here. And that's what I need. I need the kind of people involved who can raise the trust's profile. Joe is helping, of course. But it's not going to be enough. And you… You have a personal connection, as well as the, well, shall we say public appeal.'

'You mean the tabloid appeal.' Ryan remembered all too well all those headlines, all those awful photos. They felt like another life now, but to Gwen that was still who he was. And not just to Gwen. To everyone who had known him back then—including his parents.

And if he didn't do something to change that, that was who he would always be. To his family, his friends and everyone out there who read those papers. He'd come home to start over, to try and do things right this time. But he saw now that before he could do any of that he had to put to bed the person he had been.

So far, he hadn't even been able to ask for non-alcoholic beer rather than a pint when Joe asked. Or put his feelings about his brother's wife behind him.

He'd thought he'd made all the changes he needed to while he'd been in France. He'd thought he was ready to come home and show them who he was.

But now he realised that being the man he wanted to be *here*, at home in Wales, was just his next challenge.

And Gwen was giving him the chance to rise to it. Charity work, especially in his brother's memory, could be the first step to rehabilitating his character. Not just that, but if he helped Gwen…

'I'll do it,' he said, the words out of his mouth before he could think better of them. 'But on one condition. I need your help with something too.'

'My help?' Gwen stared at her brother-in-law across the table. The brief flare of elation she'd felt when he'd agreed to help faded rapidly. She couldn't imagine what Ryan could possibly need, but she was almost certain it was something she wouldn't be able to provide.

She didn't have much left to give these days. And what she had certainly hadn't been enough for his brother.

'Yeah.' Ryan looked down at the table, his voice rough. Gwen frowned. There was something about this Ryan she didn't recognise. They'd been reasonably close before he'd left, and she'd thought she'd known all there really was to know about George's little brother. But perhaps the years apart—or even his brother's death—had changed him more than she'd expected. 'I didn't just come back to Wales to play rugby for my country.'

'I thought rugby was what mattered most in the world to the Phillips boys,' Gwen joked.

Ryan didn't even smile. Instead he raised his head to meet her gaze. 'Not the only thing. Don't you remember what George used to say?'

She did, of course she did. 'Family, country, and rugby. The holy trinity of George Phillips.' Blasphemous, perhaps, but a rule he'd tried to live by when she'd met him. And while his marriage might have faded in importance as the strains and stresses had got to him, the rest of it had stuck. Until his accident, anyway.

'Exactly.' Ryan tapped fingers against the practically untouched pint in front of him. God, things must be serious if he wasn't even drinking. 'Coming home, talking to the coach today, I think I've got the last two sorted. It's the first I need your help with.'

Family. Of course.

The other thing Ryan had left behind when he'd chosen to leave the country. Gwen couldn't help but wonder what had happened to make him remember their existence now.

She studied him again in the dim light allowed by the pale wall sconces around them. He looked older, she realised. Could she hope for wiser? Probably not. George had always joked that Ryan would never change—not least because he didn't want to.

But there was a different air about him today. And that pint glass was still full.

Maybe he really was serious about this.

'What do you want me to do?' she asked, cautiously. 'No promises.'

Even that was enough to raise a tiny smile from him. 'I want to be part of Evie's life as she grows up. With George gone... I should have been there for her, and for you. A girl needs her Uncle Ryan when times are tough, right?'

'Why now?' He hadn't been here when George had been injured. When he'd changed into someone she'd barely recognised thanks to one too many bumps on the head over the years. When she'd had to hide who he'd become from their family, their friends. From Evie.

She could have used his help then. Maybe she'd even have let him see the truth.

'I... It felt like time,' he said lamely. 'I've been away long enough. And Evie's growing up—'

'Evie's been just fine the last few years,' Gwen told him bluntly. 'She doesn't even remember you, Ryan.'

'Yeah, I know. That's what made me realise... I hate the idea of her growing up not knowing me.' He stared mournfully at his pint again. 'And honestly? Maybe her Uncle Ryan needs her. And her mum. And…and her grandparents.' The pause before the last part told her he knew *exactly* how much he was asking there.

'You want me to fix things between you and your parents?' Gwen shook her head. 'I think that's *way* above my pay grade.'

'Fixing it isn't your job, Gwen. It's mine. I just need you to help me get the opportunity to do it.'

He sounded so serious, so unlike the Ryan she remembered, Gwen couldn't help but believe he truly wanted to mend fences and bring their family back together again. But he still hadn't answered the most important question she had.

'Why, Ryan? I'm serious. Why now?'

His shoulders slumped slightly at her enquiry. 'Because I can't turn back time and do it three years ago? Gwen… I've regretted how I left things here from the moment I got on that plane to France. Not leaving the team— that was the right decision for my career and my rugby skills. I learned a lot playing over there, and I'm excited to bring that knowledge back to my new team here.

'Not even leaving the country—I missed Wales, of course I did, but France has given me a lot too. So, yeah. I know I made the right decision going. But I hate how I left things here. I still have nightmares about my last conversation with my brother; he didn't understand why I needed to go and I didn't have the words to explain it to him.'

'I remember,' Gwen said softly. 'He was so angry. He thought you were leaving because of him.' He'd come upstairs and ranted for a while after Ryan had left. And when Gwen had told him that maybe it was time for Ryan to get out on his own, he'd stormed out again into the night. Gwen didn't like to think about where he'd gone, but she knew that wherever it was wore a perfume she still couldn't smell without feeling nauseous.

Ryan's silence to the accusation that he'd left because of his brother was telling, she thought. *Had* George been the reason he'd left? It couldn't have been a lot of fun living in the shadow of Wales's golden boy his whole life.

'I hate that I wasn't here when he got hurt.' Ryan's words were barely more than a whisper. 'I know that I should have been. And I hope—no, I *know*—that if I'd been on that pitch that day I'd have protected him.'

'That's what your mum always said.' Back when she'd talked about her youngest son at all. These days she seemed happiest pretending he didn't exist. At least she wasn't just complaining about his latest stint in the tabloids, Gwen supposed.

'But I wasn't. And I can't change that now.' He took a breath and straightened his shoulders, like he was preparing to defend himself. 'I can't change the things Mum and I said to each other at George's funeral either. I can't take any of it back. The past happened, and I can't change it. But I'd like to change the future, if I can.'

He sounded so earnest, so hopeful, Gwen couldn't bring herself to spell out the probable reception the idea would get back at the cottage George had bought for his parents with the proceeds of a sponsorship deal years ago.

Ryan had earned plenty with similar deals, she remembered. As far as she knew, the only beneficiaries of that money had been Cardiff's bars and clubs.

'I… I need to think about this, Ryan. Figure out the best way to approach them with this. Your parents…they're still hurting. You leaving, George's accident, then his death… it's been a lot.'

'I know.' He swallowed so hard she saw his Adam's apple bob. 'But you'll try?'

'No promises,' she said.

He shrugged. 'I'll take what I can get.'

'Okay.' She glanced down at her phone, registering the time with surprise. It was later than she'd imagined. 'But right now I need to go. I need to get home to Evie.'

'Of course.' He stood up, moving out of the booth and glancing around the bar. 'Want me to go and get Joe for you?'

She shook her head as she eased herself out of her seat. 'I'll text him. He'll understand.'

'Okay.' Hands in his pockets, he ducked his head, looking for a moment like the young man she'd first met in a Cardiff bar all those years ago, just before George had walked into her life. Except he was no fresh-faced twenty-year-old any more. He'd filled out and grown up and was all man now. Something she was trying not to notice. 'And…thanks, Gwen. Anything I can do to help with the trust I will, of course. For George. And for you and Evie.'

'I appreciate that.' She picked up her bag to leave, then paused. She didn't want to leave without giving him something. Some hope.

Ryan was right. The past was in the past and they couldn't change it. Wasn't she doing the same as him, trying to rewrite the stories that defined their lives? She was working for a better future with the trust. Didn't Ryan deserve the same chance?

'And, Ryan…' He looked up at her words, hopeful like a puppy wanting treats.

An insanely hot and muscled puppy, but still. It helped to focus on the cute factor, rather than the sexy one. One rugby player— one Phillips brother—was quite enough for one lifetime, in Gwen's opinion.

'I can't speak for your parents, or tell you how they're going to react,' she started, the words coming slowly as she thought about what she really wanted to say. 'But if you're serious about rebuilding bridges…you'll always be family to me, and to Evie. So if you want to see her, spend time with us…we can do that.'

The smile that spread across his face was every bit as bright as George's had been the day she'd said yes to the engagement ring he'd offered her.

'Really? When?'

'Um…' It had been more of a gesture than a concrete plan, but now she thought about it Gwen couldn't think of any good reason not to agree a time at least. 'Saturday?' She'd promised Evie they'd do something special together. Meeting her long lost uncle probably counted, right?

'It's a date,' Ryan said, still grinning, and Gwen ignored the way her stomach lurched at his words.

It definitely wasn't that.

She handed him her phone. 'Put your number in there. I'll text you the details.'

'And you'll talk to my parents?' he asked, as his fingers flew over the touchscreen.

'I'll try.'

'That's all any of us can do,' he replied, a wistful smile on his face.

Ryan checked the small parcel in the inside pocket of his coat one last time, and paced over to the railings to see if he could see Gwen and Evie approaching.

The text had come through late the night before, and Ryan didn't like to admit how often he'd checked his phone in the intervening days, waiting for it. He'd had a busy week of training with his new squad, settling into the new flat he'd rented, and trying to set up life back in the country of his birth. Most things—bank accounts, driving licence, et cetera—had carried on from before he'd left, but setting up a new flat and changing his address *everywhere* took more time than he'd imagined it could.

The distraction had been welcome, though.

His new team played a mere twenty miles away from the Cardiff suburb where he'd grown up, and closer still to where he knew his parents now lived. The temptation to revisit old haunts was great, and the one to show up on his parents' doorstep unannounced and try to make things right was even greater.

But he'd made a plan. He'd enlisted Gwen's help. Now he had to be guided by her on the right way to do this.

Still, when he'd received her text he'd felt a thrill go through him.

Caerphilly Castle, ten a.m. Bring chocolate buttons.

Something was happening at last. He was moving forward, not just wading through his past.

He leaned against the railings that surrounded the castle and scanned the paths around it for Gwen and Evie. It was still only just before ten; he'd been half an hour early in his eagerness. But Gwen was never late—his own tardy nature was one of the things that had driven her mad about him in the past. George had always laughed it off as just the way he was, but Gwen had been properly annoyed by it.

He couldn't risk doing *anything* to annoy her now. Well, apart from spoiling his niece a little bit too much maybe. He wondered what the gift shop had to offer…

Finally, Gwen's sleek caramel hair came into view, next to a small girl with fluffy blonde locks. Ryan felt his chest tighten at the sight; already, Evie looked so grown up compared to the baby he'd left behind. He wondered if her hair would darken to be like her dad's, in time. Wondered if she'd remember him at all. If she even remembered George.

Gwen looked up suddenly, and pointed as she spoke to Evie. The little girl looked up too, and even at such a distance Ryan saw the challenge in her bright blue eyes. George's eyes. His eyes, even.

His family.

Ryan loped down the path to meet them, his smile painfully wide as they grew closer.

'Hi.' Maybe Gwen read his nervousness— she'd always been perceptive that way—because she returned his grin with a gentle, welcoming smile of her own. Then she stepped forward, put her arms around him and hugged him.

God, she smelled good. And he knew he wasn't supposed to notice that, knew that at the least his affection for her wasn't what this day was about—even if it wasn't just all levels of wrong anyway. But he couldn't stop himself noticing it.

Ryan pulled away.

Gwen crouched down beside her daughter. 'Evie, this is your Uncle Ryan. He was your daddy's brother.'

'Hi, Evie.' Ryan gave her an awkward wave. One thing he hadn't considered in his grand plan was that he had absolutely no idea how to behave around children. In his general experience of the world, it was one thing that just hadn't come up.

Fortunately, Gwen had given him some guidance—namely the instruction to bring chocolate buttons. He'd figured that if chocolate was good, presents had to be better. And that was one thing he had actually planned ahead for.

Pulling the wrapped package from inside his coat, he held it out to Evie. 'I don't know if your mum told you, but I've been living in France the last few years. And while I was there I saw this, and it made me think of you. So I came back here to Wales to give it to you.'

Evie's eyes widened. Bouncing on her toes, she took the present from Ryan's hands, and looked up at her mother for approval.

'Yes, okay, go on, then.' Gwen rolled her eyes as Evie attacked the wrapping paper.

'You always did know how to charm the girls, Ryan.'

'This isn't actually how I used to do it,' he muttered back to her in an undertone, surprising a laugh from Gwen.

'No, I don't imagine it is.' She flashed him a look that, just for a brief moment, Ryan almost believed was flirtatious.

'It's a bunny!' Evie held the small stuffed toy up towards Gwen, who studied its fluffy little ears and stripy navy and white T-shirt with great interest.

'Not just that,' she said. 'Evie, I do believe this might be a special *French* bunny.'

Evie gasped in amazement. 'Is it, Uncle Ryan? Is it *really*?'

What the difference was between special French stuffed bunnies and regular ones, Ryan had absolutely no idea. But the little girl seemed so excited at the prospect that the only thing for it was to go along with it.

'It is. He's called Jean Paul Lapin,' he improvised.

Evie hugged the bunny close. 'I love him. Thank you, Uncle Ryan.'

'You're very welcome.' The tight feeling in his chest was familiar, Ryan thought. It felt similar, but not quite the same, to the way his body reacted when Gwen smiled at him. Like something important had just happened, even if the rest of the world never noticed.

'Shall we head up to the castle?' Gwen asked, taking Evie's hand. 'You can show Monsieur Lapin around.'

Evie's nose crinkled up in confusion. Ryan had to admit, it was kind of adorable. 'Monsor? What does that mean?'

'It's French for Mr,' Ryan explained. 'So Monsieur Lapin means Mr Rabbit.'

'Oh!' Evie's face brightened. 'Yes, I want to show Monsor Lapin my castle. And I want to show Uncle Ryan too.'

Ryan and Gwen shared a look, one that filled him with warmth and maybe, just maybe, the start of acceptance.

This, right here, was what he'd come home for.

Evie let go of her mother's hand and, Monsieur Lapin dangling from the other, grabbed Ryan's fingers instead. 'Come on,' she ordered.

Ryan had a feeling he was going to be doing what he was told a lot around Evie. 'After you, princess.'

Two hours later, and Ryan had been fully educated in every aspect of Caerphilly Castle, its history, and the best spots for playing hide and seek. Evie's energy never seemed to run out. Ryan had thought he was in peak physical condition, but apparently he had nothing on an excited almost-five-year-old.

Eventually, even Evie needed a break—and the biggest slab of chocolate brownie Ryan had ever seen. He gazed at it wistfully as he drank his herbal tea.

Gwen laughed at him. 'You know, you could have one too.'

'Not on the team diet sheet,' he said mournfully.

That made her eyebrows shoot up. 'Since when has that ever stopped *you*?'

'Since…' When had he started caring about what he needed to do for the good of the team? In France, for sure. But the changes had come so gradually it was hard to pinpoint a single moment. He shrugged. 'A while, now.'

It would have been easier if there *had* been one defining moment. One event—George's accident, perhaps, or leaving home—that had changed him. Instead, he'd had to change himself.

It was a harder road, and it took longer. But maybe he valued it more because he'd had to work for it. He hoped so.

He hoped others might too. Starting with Gwen.

Evie was fully engrossed in telling Monsieur Lapin through a spray of brownie crumbs all about the chocolate brownie and how he couldn't have any because it was bad for his teeth, and how a bunny really *needed* his teeth.

Ryan took the brief break from entertaining her—or being entertained by her, more often—to study her mother again.

Gwen had been quiet today. He'd assumed that their meeting in the hotel had been awkward because it had been the first time in so long, because they had both been asking something of the other, because it was all about the rugby—and he was sure there'd been a lot of memories of George floating around for both of them that day. But she'd been exactly the same today, quiet, reserved, almost…brittle. The Gwen he remembered had been so in love, so full of life, she'd made the world around her more colourful.

But that was before she'd lost the love of her life, of course. Stupid of him not to imagine the ways that widowhood would have changed her.

They didn't make her any less wonderful in his admittedly biased eyes, though. If anything, she was more elegant, more beautiful now, as much as he hated to think that, given what had caused it. And the depth of love in her eyes when she watched Evie... He knew that the Gwen he'd known was still there inside too.

And it did his soul so much good to see her again.

One afternoon wasn't enough, though it was a start. He was greedy. He always wanted more.

Self-restraint had been the hardest of many lessons he'd needed to learn. And in some areas he was still learning.

'I think this went well, don't you?' he asked, watching Evie as she relented and let the bunny try 'just a *tiny, tiny* bit' of the brownie. 'Us hanging out, I mean. Me being Uncle Ryan.'

'It did,' Gwen admitted. 'Better than I'd thought it would.'

'So we can do it again sometime?' He didn't want to beg, but he was sure she heard the desperation under his words all the same.

'I...' Gwen glanced between him and Evie. 'I guess that would depend on lots of things. Including how long you're around for.'

Evie's head shot up at that. 'You're not going back to France now, are you, Uncle Ryan?'

'I'm not going anywhere, Evie,' he said firmly. 'I have a contract. I'm staying here, where I can be close to my family.'

'And me?' Evie asked.

He grinned at her. 'Evie, you're the most important family I have.'

And then he tickled her, and Monsieur Lapin, for good measure.

'If she's sick, you have to clear it up,' Gwen said, dryly, but he could already tell he'd won her over.

'Next weekend, then?' he suggested, when Evie's giggles had subsided.

Gwen raised an eyebrow. 'Don't you have a match on Saturday?'

Damn. He did. His first with his new team, and not something he'd usually forget. 'I thought Sunday? I'll choose the activity this time.' Some of his new teammates had kids. He'd ask for suggestions.

She watched him for a moment, but he knew he had her. George had always said she was a soft touch when it came to under-dogs—and he was definitely that.

'Okay, fine. Sunday it is.'

CHAPTER THREE

EVIE DIDN'T LET go of Monsieur Lapin for the next two days.

It wasn't too much of a problem until Tuesday, when Gwen needed to go into Cardiff for a meeting with a potential sponsor and Evie was going to spend the day with her grandparents.

'Are you sure Monsieur Lapin wouldn't be happier at home?' Gwen asked, desperation leaking out in her words.

But Evie was her father's daughter, and as stubborn as hell when it mattered to her. 'He's my best friend. He has to come with me. Besides, I want him to meet Nain and Taid.'

Nain and Taid—the Welsh names George's mother and father had chosen for themselves as grandparents when Gwen had still been pregnant with Evie. And the two main reasons she didn't want Evie to take Monsieur Lapin, whatever excuses she'd made about worrying about him getting lost.

Her parents-in-law were totally engaged and invested in their granddaughter's life, which normally she was thrilled about. But today it would mean them noticing that Evie had a new favourite toy and asking her about it, and inevitably hearing all about Uncle Ryan.

Which was a problem. Because Gwen hadn't quite found the right way to talk to them about their prodigal son's return just yet.

They might already know, she'd reasoned. They kept up with the sport their sons loved even now. They might have been watching the championship final. In fact, she knew they had, because they'd texted to say they'd seen her with Joe on the big screen afterwards. Maybe they'd spotted Ryan too. Or maybe they'd seen the announcement of his transfer back to Wales in the press the next day.

But they hadn't mentioned it if they had. Which meant that, even if they knew, they were trying to ignore it.

Perhaps they were waiting for him to come to them, but Gwen doubted it.

She loved her in-laws dearly. But she also knew they were wrong about Ryan.

There was nothing for it now, anyway. She

had to get to her meeting, and Evie wasn't going anywhere without Monsieur Lapin.

She dropped Evie off with her nain and taid with only the barest greeting and fare-well—and the promise to stay for dinner when she got back to make up for it. As the front door closed behind her, she heard her mother-in-law saying, 'And who is this fine fellow, now?' and winced.

Then she put the whole thing out of her head until later. She had business to do, meet-ings to concentrate on. And thinking about Ryan Phillips was not good for her concen-tration, it seemed.

But as she pulled her car into Meredith and Dylan Phillips' driveway later that afternoon, she knew she couldn't ignore any of it any longer. She'd made an agreement with Ryan, and she had to hold up her part of it. Espe-cially after today's meetings.

'How did it go?' her father-in-law, Dylan, asked as he opened the door to her. Another point in their favour, they were totally sup-portive of her work setting up George's trust. It was enough to make her feel guilty for even *talking* to Ryan again. Which was insane. Whatever Meredith said, however much they resented the fact that Ryan had left, George's accident hadn't been his fault. And his death certainly hadn't been.

'So-so.' She shrugged off her coat. 'People like the idea, they want to help, but they need more visibility before they'll help me become more visible. If that makes any sense at all.'

'Not much,' Dylan said cheerfully. 'Come on, love. There's Bolognese on the stove, and I'll pour you a glass of wine. That'll make it all look better.'

'How's Evie been?' she asked, as they moved through the hallway towards the lounge at the back of the house.

'Fine, fine.' But he shot her a quick look as he said it that suggested that it hadn't all been quite as *fine* as he said. 'I think her nain is looking at some old albums with her right now. She wanted to see her Uncle Ryan apparently.'

Gwen's chest tightened. Here it was, time to come clean. But, really, what was there to say other than Ryan was in town and had asked to see Evie? She hadn't done anything wrong.

So why did it feel like she had?

Dylan grabbed a wine glass from the kitchen on the way past and pressed it into her hand, filling it with wine almost to the brim.

'Thanks.' She had a feeling she was going to need it.

'I'd better stir the Bolognese,' he said, retreating. Dylan never had liked conflict.

George and Ryan both got their fighting spirit from their mother, it seemed.

Taking a swig of the wine, Gwen moved to the doorway to the lounge to watch Evie and her nain.

'And this is your daddy scoring his first try for his country,' Meredith was saying, as she turned the page of an old-fashioned photo album. 'Do you remember how many he scored altogether, *cariad bach*?'

'Thirty-two,' Evie recited dutifully. 'That's right, isn't it, Nain?'

'It is,' Meredith said proudly.

'How many did Uncle Ryan score?' Evie asked, and Gwen watched Meredith's expression darken.

Time to intervene.

'Hello, you two! Have you been having fun today?'

'Mummy!' Evie spun around and launched herself at Gwen. 'Monsieur Lapin missed you!'

'Did he? How about you? Did you miss me?' She pressed a kiss to Evie's soft, blonde hair.

'A little bit,' Evie said, after some consideration. 'But I was having fun with Nain and Taid.' She dropped her voice. 'I don't think Nain likes Monsieur Lapin, though.'

Of course she didn't. 'Why don't you go and help Taid in the kitchen?' she suggested to Evie. 'You know he always stirs the sauce the wrong way.'

'And never grates enough cheese!' Evie agreed, skipping off to correct her grandfather's culinary mistakes.

In her chair, Meredith slammed the photo album closed. 'So. You've seen Ryan, I hear?'

Okay, so there was no gentling into this conversation, then. Gwen dropped into the nearest chair, and took another gulp of wine. From the tone of her mother-in-law's voice, she was going to need it.

'I bumped into him at the match,' she started, leaving out the part where she'd actually gone to the bar to seek him out. 'He's moved back to Wales for good, did you know?'

'His father might have seen something about it on the internet,' Meredith admitted. 'But since he didn't let us know himself, we weren't sure it was true.'

'He wanted to see Evie,' Gwen told her. 'And he wanted me to talk to you and Dylan before he came to see you both.'

Meredith stiffened at that. 'He can't face his own parents like a man and apologise for what he did?'

What he did? Or what he said? Gwen wondered. Was Meredith really still angry about the things they'd said to each other at George's funeral, or just still unable to forgive Ryan for leaving in the first place, for not being there to protect his brother on the pitch? She suspected the latter.

'He wants to come and see you and apologise. Rebuild bridges, he said. Would you be open to that?'

Meredith looked down at the album in her hands, spreading it open again to a page filled with press photographs and newspaper clippings. All about George, of course. Gwen suspected there must be a similar album for Ryan somewhere, but she'd certainly never seen it since he'd left.

'What kind of mother would I be if I didn't see my son?' she asked softly. But she was still staring at the photos of George, tracing his face with her finger.

Gwen bit the inside of her cheek, uncertain. This didn't look like forgiveness. This looked like punishment.

George's parents still clung so tightly to the past—to who George had been before his accident. Maybe she'd hidden the changes in him afterwards too well. Or maybe they just hadn't wanted to see it. Wilful, blissful ignorance.

But not everyone was willing or able to do that. She'd hidden it well from the people close to her, but George had had other friends, other acquaintances, that she'd never known. Like the woman with the heavy perfume, or the people who had been with him the night he'd died. She'd never met any of them.

There were enough people out there who knew the truth about who George had become, and who had no loyalty to her to hide it. She lived in fear of an exposé one day, on the anniversary of his death perhaps. Evie was learning to read now. If there were headlines, with photos of her father, and she saw them…

Maybe she couldn't keep the truth from her for ever, but she could change the story. Make it about the good that came from tragedy. With Ryan's help.

And he needed her help too. She'd seen that the other day, at the castle. The desperately hopeful smile on his face as he'd handed Evie the bunny had told her all she needed to know.

Helping Ryan, and Ryan helping her, was

the right thing to do. No matter how difficult it might be to start with.

Meredith was still staring at the photos of George.

'I'll arrange with Ryan to get together one day soon, then, shall I?' she asked.

Meredith didn't look up. 'Whatever you think best, dear.'

Fine. That's what she'd been doing ever since even before George's accident. She'd just keep on going, and hope for the best.

What else was there to do?

When Ryan saw the text message from Gwen a mere two days later, his heart lurched in his chest.

'Message from your girlfriend, Ry?' Dewi asked, across the changing room. Being in the same club as his friend had played a large part in Ryan's decision to sign on with the Selkies, rather than one of the other, more famous Welsh teams, but for the first time he was starting to regret it. Dewi was a notorious gossip, and if he thought there was something interesting going on in Ryan's life, he wouldn't stop asking until he found out what it was.

Ryan slipped his phone into his pocket, planning to reply to the message later. 'Nothing half as interesting, I'm afraid, mate. Just a family obligation.'

His parents weren't the sort to air dirty laundry in public—one of the things his mum had hated most about his wilder days was how they had been documented online and in print, so everyone knew exactly what disgraceful behaviour he'd been up to, and with whom. Ryan felt pretty sure that the extent of his estrangement from his family wouldn't be common knowledge because he hadn't told anyone—and he couldn't imagine his parents doing so. If he got his way it would all be mended before anyone ever had to know about it. All the same, it felt wrong describing Gwen as an obligation.

At least until he actually read the text message, and realised what she was asking him to do.

He met her at the hospital the next day anyway, just as she'd asked. Because apparently he was still no good at saying no to Gwen.

'Care to tell me exactly what we're doing here?' he asked, as they strode through the hospital corridors. He tried to guess where they were going from signage on the walls, but the place was so large and sprawling she could have been leading him anywhere.

'You'll see,' she replied.

Ryan tried to hold in a shudder as the hospital smell became overwhelming, the deeper they got. As a rugby player, he was no stranger to hospital wards, although he'd been lucky enough to mostly be patched up by the team doctors. Not many rugby players could get as far in their careers as he had without succumbing to some sort of major injury—the sort that put a player out for months, a whole season, a year, or for ever. George certainly hadn't.

'As long as you're not taking me to the STI clinic,' he joked, trying to lighten the mood. Ever since they'd met in the car park Gwen had been quiet and reserved, in a way he'd hoped they'd moved past at the castle on Saturday. Apparently not.

She shot him a scathing glance. 'Of course that's the only part of the hospital you're familiar with.'

It wasn't true, though, was it? Ryan thought, striding alongside her down the endless corridors. Quite aside from his own injuries, he'd been in this very hospital when George had been hurt. Sat terrified by his brother's bed, waiting to see if he'd wake up.

He'd been in France when the accident had happened, watching his home team play on a foreign television screen, cheering them on all the way. Even his teammates, who might normally have favoured Italy over Wales, had been shouting support for the boys in red. The room had been rowdy and alive—and had fallen instantly silent the moment George had been tackled.

It wasn't even an illegal tackle, that was the hardest thing to process. It was a perfectly normal, run-of-the-mill tackle, the sort George dodged or survived every game, multiple times. The sort Ryan himself made regularly. The exact sort he was known for, actually.

But rugby was a contact sport, and every player knew the risks. He'd played with a lad once, in the under-eighteens team, who'd fallen badly after a tackle and severed his spinal cord. Left with no feeling in his legs at all.

They all knew the risks.

But they all also, secretly, believed that they were too good to fall. That the training, the hard work, the drive and the ambition would keep them alive. They couldn't play if they didn't.

George was luckier than some. He slammed into the ground at a bad angle, unable to turn, gripping the ball too tightly to put his hands

out to save himself. He landed awkwardly
on his arm and shoulder—they could all see
that from the camera angles. Then his head
had bounced off the turf—no mud and rain
to soften it, for once—and his eyes had rolled
back.

Over in France, Ryan had been on in his
feet in an instant, and on a plane home almost
before the full-time whistle blew.

Ryan shook the memories away, and focussed on where Gwen was taking him. The
corridors were familiar, the doors, the art-
work… He realised belatedly she was leading him towards the department where they'd
sat with George's doctor after the accident,
learning about what to expect next.

Gwen knocked on the door, and he recognised the name, printed on a brass plaque.
A. Chowdhury. The surgeon who'd treated
George. Not the one who'd put the bolts in his
arm to hold it together. The one who'd dealt
with his head injury.

'Gwen! So good to see you.' The woman
who opened the door and embraced Gwen
was petite, quick moving and, on their previous acquaintance, the smartest person Ryan
had ever met. 'How is Evie?'

She motioned them inside, smiling at Ryan
as she indicated for them both to sit.

'Evie's great, thanks. Currently obsessed with a toy rabbit her Uncle Ryan brought her from France.'

'Ah, yes.' Anita Chowdhury turned her chocolate-brown eyes towards him, and Ryan tried not to squirm under the directness of her gaze. It was hard to make his six-foot-two frame inconspicuous, though, especially in such a small room. 'George's brother Ryan. I remember you.'

'Thank you for everything you did for my brother,' he said.

The doctor inclined her head in acceptance. 'George's injury was terribly unfortunate. But it brought Gwen into our world. And I think she's going to make a real difference to a lot of other people's lives.' She turned back to Gwen. 'You wanted to run over the details for the fundraiser?'

Gwen shook her head. 'It's all in hand, I think. You have your invitations?'

'And my party frock sorted,' Anita confirmed. 'But if not the fundraiser, why did you want to see me?'

Gwen glanced across at him, and suddenly Ryan knew. This was about him.

'I was hoping you could talk to my brother-in-law here about the work you do, and the impact we want the trust to have. He's moving home to Wales, so I'm hoping he can help us raise our profile—but that means he has to know what he's talking about.'

Ryan frowned, and twisted to face her, speaking in an undertone. 'I didn't sign up for some medical crash course, Gwen. I know about head injuries—every rugby player does. And even if they didn't, I saw what happened to George.'

It hadn't just been the head injury, of course, although that had been the scariest part. It had been the damage to his arm and shoulder that had put an end to his rugby career. If a player couldn't catch a ball reliably, he was no good out on the field. And George's range of movement had been so limited by his injury, no one had seriously believed he could play again.

'Did you?' Anita asked, her eyebrows raised under her dark, curly hair. 'You saw him unconscious, yes? But I imagine that once he awoke, you assumed he was back to normal again?'

Beside him, Gwen stiffened slightly, but before Ryan could figure out what had triggered her reaction the doctor was talking again.

'I see more than my share of rugby players here, and most of them seem to feel that taking five minutes off the pitch for the head injury assessment is more than adequate for protecting players. It isn't.'

'Most of us *do* know that,' Ryan put in. 'There just isn't much we can do about it.'

Frustration coloured Anita's expression. 'Well, there *should* be. Even a mild concussion has serious consequences. Repeated concussions, not to mention more severe head injuries…' She shook her head. 'The list of effects is too long for me to list them all. But let's start with the possibility of severe brain damage, affecting neurocognitive deficits, and work backwards through delusions, weakness of limbs, loss of co-ordination, personality changes, aggression, convulsions, slurred speech, confusion, amnesia—'

'Okay, okay. I get it,' Ryan said. 'Brain injuries aren't something to be taken lightly. That's why Gwen is trying to raise money for people who suffer them, right?'

'It's a life-changing injury,' Gwen said softly. 'In so many ways, and for everyone around the person. People need support—and I want to give it to them.'

That darkness was back behind her eyes. How hard had it been for her, supporting George's recovery, looking after Evie, dealing with their parents…? Ryan had been back on the plane to France as soon as they'd known that George would live. But now he wondered: had his brother been more affected by his injuries than he knew? And how?

Having to give up the career he loved must have been impossibly hard for George. But dealing with a body that wouldn't do what he wanted? Ryan knew from past injuries how frustrating that could be too.

But he'd had Gwen to support him. Not everyone could be that lucky. George had always been the lucky one. But had Gwen?

'Then I want to help you.' Ryan held her gaze, and she nodded. Then he turned back to the doctor. 'Okay. I'm listening. What else do I need to know?'

Three days later, Gwen fastened the diamond necklace that George had given her the day he'd got called up for the Lions tour around her neck, then sighed at her reflection in the mirror of her hotel room.

She looked tired. She knew she looked tired, and there was only so much that concealer could do. George's parents had mentioned it when she'd dropped Evie off for her sleepover. And that meant that Ryan was bound to notice, and comment on it. Her brother-in-law had never had much in the way of tact.

But what was she supposed to tell him? *I can't sleep because I'm having nightmares about you and your brother.*

Except that wasn't technically true. However wildly inappropriate the dreams might be, she couldn't really classify them as nightmares.

They'd started the day Ryan had come back into her life, and they'd only intensified with every extra minute they spent together. As if he was worming his way into her subconscious somehow.

The first night she'd dreamt of the day they'd met—that Cardiff bar she'd visited with friends. Ryan had burst across the room to sit with her, flirt with her, before getting distracted by a tray of shots his friend had been offering and wandering off again. He'd been a whirlwind of charm and good looks and the kind of smile that had made things inside her melt—but even then Gwen had never considered him anything but a few minutes' entertainment on a night out.

In reality, George had approached her moments later, apologising for his brother's lack of manners. He'd bought her a drink, they'd talked all evening—and the rest was history.

Her dreams didn't seem to accept that, though. In her dreams it wasn't George who came over but this new Ryan, returned from France, older and steadier—and, she had to admit, even hotter than he'd been as a careless young twenty-year-old.

The first few nights she'd woken up when she'd realised the man sitting down with her wasn't George. Then one night she hadn't. And after that the dreams had changed.

Now, when she dreamt, she was always lying somewhere warm and cosy, firelight in the background, blankets around her. And she was naked. She blushed at the memory. Always naked.

Then she'd feel someone behind her—someone who made her feel safe, warm and loved. He'd run his hands up over her bare skin, skirting over every inch of her sensitive body, his lips against her shoulder, her neck, her ear. Her whole body would tremble with need as she'd feel him hard against her lower back. *I need you*, she'd whisper. And he'd comply.

His hands at her breasts, he'd push gently inside her, filling her, making her whole body clench around him. As they moved together, she'd feel everything in her growing tighter, closer…

And then, just before she reached her peak, she'd turn to look at the man behind her. She'd twist and see the dark hair, the blue eyes she knew so very well. *George*. Then the firelight would flicker and she'd realise she was wrong.

It was Ryan. It always turned out to be Ryan.

That shock woke her up, every time. She'd come to, sitting upright in her bed, alone, her body tight with desperate want, cursing her unconscious brain.

Why? Why was she dreaming of *Ryan*?

She didn't want to give too much power, or meaning, to dreams. Ryan was almost a carbon copy of his older brother—an inch or two shorter, perhaps, a little broader in the shoulder, carrying a little more muscle. His eyes sparkled with more amusement at the world than George's ever had, but otherwise they were alike enough to be confused on and off the pitch, unless a person could see their shirt number.

Maybe it just meant it had been too long since she'd had sex—with anybody. Maybe it meant she had a type—dark hair, blue eyes, built like a rugby player. Because since that very first night they'd met she knew she'd never looked at Ryan this way. Not once, when George had been alive.

But now, after these dreams, it was getting so much harder not to. Hard to remember him as her reckless, unreliable brother-in-law.

Especially since he'd been neither of those things since he'd returned.

Gwen didn't know quite *who* he was now. But she could at least admit to herself that she wanted to find out.

She took a deep breath, threaded the matching diamond earrings through her lobes, and gave herself one last smile in the mirror. Her caramel highlighted hair sat neatly against her collar bone, above the draping neckline of her gold evening dress.

She looked exactly like what she supposed she was. A wealthy widow looking to find a way to make a positive impact on the world. To matter. To provide her husband with the legacy she hoped he deserved.

She just didn't look all that much like Gwen Phillips, the woman she had been, before everything had changed. The woman she still hoped she was, inside.

Tonight was the night of the charity fundraiser she'd set up in conjunction with the hospital, and another charity focussing on head injuries. Gwen knew there was often competition between charities for donors and support, but in her mind as long as the money was getting to the people that needed it she was doing her job right. The George Phillips Trust was more about helping people than anything else, using the profile the name gave them to reach people who might not otherwise have engaged with the problem.

Ryan, at least, seemed engaged. She'd worried if she was doing the right thing, taking him to see Anita. If the doctor had let something slip, let on about the personality changes George had suffered…she didn't want Ryan burdened with that knowledge too. Let him remember his brother as he was—the golden, shining man they'd both loved.

But Anita had known what she was doing. She'd patiently taken him through the work she did, and some anonymous case studies of patients who'd suffered traumatic brain injuries of all levels, and with various effects. Ryan, to his credit, had listened attentively, nodding along and only speaking to ask insightful questions that provided more clarity. Even Gwen, who'd been studying the subject for years now, had felt more educated after the session.

'Okay,' he'd said, as Anita had brought things to an end so she could get back to her *actual* work. 'I get it. Well, I mean, I know I have a hell of a lot more to learn, but I understand the importance, I think. And I definitely want to help. So what can I do?'

'Well,' Anita had replied, 'we do need one more volunteer for our charity fundraiser.'

'I'll do it,' Ryan had agreed easily, apparently unaware of the mischievous look Anita had shot Gwen's way. Or the panic that had surged through Gwen at the very idea.

Still, neither of them had enlightened Ryan as to the actual nature of the fundraiser. Gwen figured she'd save that for when he was already there, and couldn't run away. He would, she had to admit, make the perfect addition to their bachelor auction line up.

But imagining that was when the dreams had changed from the bar to the fireside, damn it. Which was why Gwen had decided to blame Anita for the whole thing—even if she wasn't telling her friend about them. Or anyone else, for that matter.

There was a knock on the hotel-room door, and Gwen crossed to open it, with just one last glance at the mirror to check how bad the shadows under her eyes really looked.

'Hey, are you okay?' Ryan asked, the minute she opened the door. Which told her more than the mirror ever could.

'Just tired. Evie's been waking up at night. Nightmares, I think.' She felt bad lying to him, and worse for using her daughter as an excuse, but really it had to be better than confessing the truth, right?

I can't sleep because every time I close my eyes I imagine you naked.

Not a great conversation starter. At least, not when the subject of it was her brother-in-law.

However desperate her body apparently was for some physical human contact, Ryan was the last man she could consider asking to scratch that itch.

'Well, a glass of wine and a bit of a party should perk you right up.' Ryan offered her his arm. 'If you're ready, my lady.'

Gwen checked her room key in her clutch bag, then took his arm.

'So, what's my job tonight?' Ryan asked, as they waited for the elevator. 'Do you want me schmoozing the rich kids for donations? Or am I here as a cautionary tale about the risks of too many hits to the head playing rugby?'

Gwen winced. This was probably the time to tell about the bachelor auction, she supposed.

'Actually...' she started, but then the elevator door opened, revealing Anita Chowdhury in a gorgeous red and gold evening gown.

She was accompanied by several women that Gwen recognised from hospital wards.

'Ah, here he is, ladies.' Anita reached out to grab Ryan's arm and yank him into the elevator. 'The star of our bachelor auction tonight.'

Ryan's eyebrows jumped towards his hairline. Gwen stepped into the elevator behind him and pressed the button for the lobby.

'Bachelor auction?' Ryan asked, his voice a little higher and squeakier than normal.

'I was about to tell you,' Gwen said. The elevator started to move as the other occupants began peppering Ryan with questions—about his rugby career, about France, and his relationship status.

He was out of the elevator the minute the doors opened again. Gwen turned to Anita and rolled her eyes. Anita just smirked.

'Oh, dear,' she said. 'I hope you brought your purse, Gwen. Looks like you might need to save our reluctant bachelor.'

Gwen looked towards Ryan, already most of the way to the bar and chatting with a selection of hangers-on she recognised from the rugby circuit. 'I think he can manage just fine on his own.'

'I'm sure he can,' Anita said. 'But I'm pretty certain there's only one woman here he wants bidding on him tonight.'

Gwen jerked her head round to stare at her friend. 'What do you mean?'

'The way you look tonight? You can't tell me you haven't noticed the way he's been staring at you.'

'He thinks I look tired. Besides, we were in a tiny cramped elevator. Where else is he supposed to look?' But saying it didn't make Gwen forget the way his eyes had roamed over her dress as she'd answered the door. Or the way that every time she'd looked at him lately he'd always seemed to be looking back.

Maybe he was suffering from hugely inappropriate dreams too.

'Fine. Deny it if you want. But you can't tell me that man sat in my office and listened to the gory details of traumatic brain injuries for the sake of his own health.' Anita raised one perfectly arched eyebrow at her. 'Or even for his brother's memory. Trust me, Gwen, if he's doing this, he's doing it for you.'

Gwen shook her head. 'You're wrong. He's doing this for his family—or rather to get his family back. I'm just the means to an end.'

Then Ryan turned around and smiled at her, and Gwen felt all the same heat she remembered from her dreams flooding through her as his gaze locked onto hers.

Anita looked between them. 'Yeah. Of course he is.' She patted Gwen gently on the arm. 'You just keep telling yourself that. Now, let's go get a glass of nice, cold champagne. You look like you need cooling down.'

CHAPTER FOUR

A BACHELOR AUCTION. Of course.

Time was, Ryan would have seen this as an opportunity. A chance to bask in the attention of women who wanted him—rather than the one who didn't. Maybe even the chance to catch the eye of someone to take home for the night.

Today, though, there was only one woman he wanted bidding on him. And she categorically wasn't.

He was up fourth in a line-up of six. After him there was a reality TV star and a celebrity chef; before him a local councillor, a runner up from a TV talent show, a well-known business star and the best-looking surgeon the hospital had been able to talk into taking part. Which at least let Ryan know where he was in the scale of biddability.

Except all the others clearly had people in the crowd there to drive their bidding up.

Ryan only had Gwen who, when it was his turn on stage, stood with her arms folded over her chest, staring at the auctioneer rather than him.

Great.

His monkey suit felt too tight around his neck, the bow-tie too flashy, the shirt too starched. He had a match to play tomorrow. He should be home preparing, resting. Not standing on stage being bid for like an expensive antique vase.

Except Gwen needed him to. So there he was.

'And next up we have a very special addition to our line-up!' The auctioneer—a woman in a tight black dress and skyscraper heels who seemed to be having far too much fun at their expense—flashed another naughty smile at the crowd. 'I'm sure all you rugby fans out there know who he is without introduction, but for the rest of you, let me introduce Ryan Phillips!' A smattering of applause—and a whoop Ryan suspected came from Anita Chowdhury.

'Ex-Wales player, he's been over in France playing his rugby for the last few years, but now he's back! And we were lucky enough to snag him before even the Welsh rugby team could.' She glanced down at her notes. 'Ryan says he likes sharing a bottle of wine by candlelight, nights out on the town, and going for a run on the beach.'

Ryan had most definitely never said any of those things. He suspected Gwen's hand behind those words. He shot her a look and found her, for once, looking at him—at least until she caught his eye and looked away rapidly.

'Shall we start the bidding at fifty pounds? Who will pay fifty for a night out with this fine gentleman?'

She wasn't entirely wrong either, Ryan mused, as the bidding started. He *did* like running on the beach—Gwen would have remembered that from back when he and George had trained together. And back then, a night out on the town had been the highlight of his week, even when George had turned them down because of training. She wouldn't know that he'd changed, in that respect. That he'd finally learned the lesson his brother had spent years trying to teach him—that if he wanted to be the best he had to give everything to the game, to his training. And that meant following the rules and sacrificing some fun sometimes.

But it was the first item on the list that interested him most. Sharing a bottle of wine by candlelight? He could almost imagine it now—that kind of private, intimate evening with Gwen. Had she been imagining it when she'd written that?

He sneaked another look at her. She was staring at her phone.

No. He couldn't let himself start hoping for that kind of attention from Gwen. She'd probably been thinking of George when she'd written it. She'd never even seen him drink wine.

Probably wouldn't now, given how rarely he drank anything alcoholic at all.

'And sold!' the auctioneer said. 'At one thousand, three hundred pounds, to the lady in the *beautiful* purple frock.'

Not a bad number, Ryan decided. More than the businessman had gone for, and the surgeon. He glanced over at the woman who'd won him, celebrating with her friends. He sighed. She was no Gwen, but for charity he could definitely manage a nice evening out for her. He'd have to go talk to her, find out what sort of thing she liked.

Then he was going to find Gwen.

The lady in purple—Rachel, it transpired—was an avid rugby fan.

'I mean, I loved your brother—God rest his

soul—and I wish I'd got to meet him. But a night out with you is pretty great too!'

Of course. Had he ever been anything but a poor substitute for his brother?

'I'm looking forward to it too,' Ryan lied, with a smile. 'Now, why don't you let me have your number and I'll call to make plans soon. That way you can enjoy the rest of your evening with your friends.' He indicated the gaggle of giggling women behind her.

They giggled some more.

'Maybe we can all join you for your night out,' one of them suggested.

Rachel scowled. 'Not unless you want to pay your share!'

'I'll let you ladies decide this between yourselves,' Ryan said, and slipped away.

The ballroom of the hotel was decked out with lights and ribbons, along with some banners for the charity, and information tables. It certainly wasn't the swankiest or highest-profile fundraiser he'd ever been to, but it did at least have plenty of connections to and information on the cause it was raising money for. And it had Gwen, which made it hit his top ten automatically.

He found her loitering by an information stand, where Anita Chowdhury was talking at length with two attendees. He smiled as he recognised one of the two men—Joe and, he assumed, his husband.

Gwen didn't seem too involved in the conversation, though, so he figured he could wait and greet Joe and Ben later. He wanted to talk to her alone first.

Moving behind her, he touched one hand to Gwen's waist. She flinched.

Swallowing his disappointment at her reaction, Ryan said, 'Come get a drink with me?'

She nodded, and together they moved towards the bar outside the ballroom on the other side of the hotel lobby. It was quieter there, and he'd noticed she preferred that these days. Even in the crowded ballroom, at a fundraiser she'd organised, she'd clung to the walls.

Presumably that was why she needed people like him involved. To talk to donors when she wouldn't.

'So,' he said, as she hopped up onto the stool at the farthest end of the bar, 'apparently I'm having dinner with Rachel in the purple dress, and possibly several of her friends, soon. She'd have preferred George, she tells me, but under the circumstances it seems that I'll do.'

Gwen looked down at the bar, but he could tell that she was smiling. 'Sorry.'

'No, you're not,' he challenged. 'You think it's hilarious.' Because it *was* hilarious, in lots of ways.

Or it would be, if it were happening to somebody else.

She peeked up from under her eyelashes, and he saw amusement dancing in her eyes. Good. At least he could still make her laugh, that was something.

'I hope it's not too awful,' she said.

Ryan shrugged. 'I'll have been on worse dates, I'm sure.'

They ordered drinks—gin and tonic for her, an alcohol-free beer for him—and waited for the bartender to move away again before they started talking.

'So you're not too cross with me for offering you up as a sacrifice to the auction gods and goddesses?' Gwen took a sip of her drink.

'I never could stay cross with you,' he admitted.

She flashed him a quick smile. 'I'd have thought that dozens of beautiful women bidding for your time and your body was basically your dream, isn't it?'

'It might have been once,' Ryan admitted. 'But I'm not the same man I was when I left Wales, you know.'

The smile slipped away from her face as

she looked up at him. 'No,' she said, thought-fully. 'I don't think you are, are you?'

His heartbeat stuttered at her words. Did she really believe that?

He knew she hadn't thought it when they'd first met again. She'd assumed he'd be ex-actly the same Ryan who'd left them all be-hind years ago.

Ryan hoped—knew—that he'd changed. But knowing it wasn't the same as other peo-ple believing it. But if Gwen believed, maybe others could too.

Maybe even his parents.

His mother had never been able to see past the golden boy George to notice *him*—not re-ally. And the more he'd gone out of his way to *make* her pay him attention, the less he'd been the son she'd wanted at all. He'd seen that, finally, even if it had taken him a while.

But things were different now. Weren't they? *He* was different.

'Moving to France, it gave me a chance to re-evaluate a lot of things.' Ryan toyed with the neck of his beer bottle. He wondered if she'd even noticed the zero per cent alcohol label. Probably not. People, in his experience, seemed to see exactly what they expected to see. Quitting drinking almost completely was just one more change he'd made to try and become the man he wanted to be. Focussed on his training, sharp of mind. Not to mention the fact that the hangovers got more killer the older he got. 'I mean, I didn't speak the language, I was in a strange country where I didn't know anybody. Kind of gave me a lot of time to think, you know?'

'I know.' Gwen stared down at her drink. 'In some ways… It was the same after George's accident, and again after he died. More so after the funeral. In between there was so much to deal with—hospital appointments, physio exercises, helping Evie understand what was going on. And even after his death there was the funeral to arrange, newspapers banging on the door, and the police investigation. But once that was all over… It was just me, and Evie, and your parents, trying to figure out how to live now. Friends didn't know what say, so they didn't say anything at all. And you weren't here…'

'I'm sorry about that.' Ryan reached across the table and grabbed her hand. 'If it had happened before I moved to France, maybe it would have changed things. But I was committed, I had contracts, obligations. And I was building a new life for myself.'

Gwen's gaze flickered up to meet his. 'Your

mother thought it must be a woman keeping you over there, you know?'

Ryan barked a laugh. The sad thing was, in a way his mother was right. Except he hadn't been running back to a woman in France. He'd been running away from what he couldn't have, right here in Wales.

He dropped Gwen's hand.

One he still couldn't have.

She was so close right now, anyone watching them must think they were couple—or at least on their way to becoming one. If this were a date he'd lean across the table and tuck her hair behind her ear. He'd speak softly so she'd move closer to hear. He'd angle his head just right so all she had to do was move in and they'd be kissing.

And for a moment, sitting there, he could almost believe that she would.

Maybe. One day. Soon?

No. He couldn't let his hopes rise that way, even if she gave him cause. Gwen belonged to George and she always would. He could handle being a poor second prize to his brother for Rachel in the purple dress.

It would break him to be that consolation price for Gwen. He couldn't even let himself consider it. The temptation—to be anything she wanted, even a George substitute

if it meant he got to touch her, kiss her, stay
in her life—was too great. And he'd worked
too hard to be his own person.

He couldn't give that up now just because
his heart stopped when she smiled at him.

Ryan picked up his beer and got to his
feet. 'Come on. We're missing the party.' He
was done tormenting himself with things he
couldn't have.

Gwen fastened Evie's coat right to the top,
then shoved her own hands in her pockets.
The stadium might be packed, but it was still
freezing in the cold March wind. Beside her,
she could hear Meredith muttering about why
they had to be there. Gwen didn't think they'd
been to a rugby match since George's accident, although she knew they still watched
them all on the telly. George's accident might
have been career ending, but as far as they
were concerned it hadn't been the cause of his
death. Rugby was rugby, and nothing would
change that for them.

However differently she might feel about
the repercussions of that accident, Gwen
couldn't deny the thrill that still went through
her as she saw the teams running out from
the tunnel. Ryan's first match starting for his

new team, the Selkies. It seemed as good a time as any to reintroduce him to his parents.

She'd never fully understood the relationship between Ryan and his parents—especially his mother. Over the years when Ryan had still lived in Wales, Meredith had cried and despaired of her youngest son's exploits, and the disrepute he'd brought on the family name. Gwen would have thought that Ryan taking his bad behaviour and reputation overseas would be a good thing, in some ways—but it had only made Meredith more furious.

Gwen remembered asking George about it at the time, but he'd only shrugged, his own anger with his brother still raw.

'He's supposed to be here, with us,' he'd said simply. *'He's part of the team. His place is out there on the pitch with me.'*

She'd known what he'd meant by that. Ryan's job on the team was setting up tries for George to score, turning over the ball then passing it to his brother to take the glory. They had worked so well together, in perfect synchronicity. Always had.

But how had it felt for Ryan to always be the one in the background? To be the disappointment, the black sheep? She'd always thought he'd revelled in it a bit. But now, seeing the man he'd become outside his brother's shadow, she wondered.

She had missed him, of course, while he'd been away. As she and George had become serious about each other, Ryan had been a big part of her life, along with his parents. He was the younger brother who'd steal extra pudding with her after Sunday lunch, who she'd find asleep on their sofa after a team night out. He'd made a great cooked breakfast, and had always had time to listen to her over a cup of tea when she'd been worried about George, or Evie, or anything.

He'd gone out and bought an 'I have the world's best uncle' onesie for Evie, the day they'd told him they were expecting. He'd always, always been there, and she'd felt the loss of him desperately when he'd gone away.

But she'd never been angry about it. It wasn't her place to make choices for him after all. She had no hold over Ryan, never had. And neither did anyone else.

Even after George's accident, after Ryan's flying visit home, she'd not been angry. There had been nights when she'd wished, desperately, that he was still there—that she could call him to come round for a cup of tea and offload everything onto his broad shoulders.

That he could come back and be the brother he'd always been to them, part of the team.

But as George's behaviour had become more erratic, angrier and even more hurtful, part of her had been glad Ryan hadn't been there to see it.

'There's Uncle Ryan!' Evie shouted now. Around them, people turned to see who had a relative out there on the pitch. Meredith looked a little flustered and embarrassed, but Ryan's dad stood a little straighter, a little prouder. Having a rugby player in the family, especially a professional one, still meant an awful lot here in Wales.

'I can see him,' Gwen said to her daughter.

'Do you think if I wave he'll see me?' Evie asked.

Gwen looked around at the crowds. It wasn't like an international match, where every seat was filled with fans singing and chanting, but there was still a decent crowd here to see the boys play. 'You can try, but Uncle Ryan has to focus on his game.'

Behind her, Gwen heard a man snigger and mutter, 'Can't see why he'd start now, when he never bothered before. Don't know why the coach signed him.' Apparently Ryan's reputation as a wild card still carried around here.

Gwen's jaw tightened as she resisted the

urge to respond, to tell the guy he didn't know what he was talking about.

Even before he'd left for France, Ryan had cared about his rugby. He might not have had the dedication of his brother or the single-minded focus his coach would have liked, but he'd cared. And since he'd come back, well, even Gwen had to admit he seemed to have grown up a lot. Just talking to him last night at the fundraiser had shown her that. He genuinely wanted to help her with the trust, and was dedicated enough to learn, to listen, and even to date Rachel in the purple dress.

It had shown her other things too, but Gwen wasn't thinking about those right now. Definitely not that moment when she'd thought, for a second, that he'd been about to kiss her.

That way madness lay.

Better to focus on the game ahead of them. And how she was going to reconcile Ryan with his parents afterwards.

Meredith had been reluctant when she'd suggested meeting Ryan for lunch after the match, but Dylan had agreed for both of them—one of the few times in Gwen's memory that he'd made a decision without deferring to his wife first. That gave her hope. Even if Meredith was still angry with Ryan—an anger Gwen didn't fully understand—at least his father seemed open to a reconciliation.

As long as the right Ryan showed up for lunch. That was her main concern. The man she'd got to know again since his return was ready to mend fences and fix the broken relationship—and she had faith he could do it. But there had always been something about the relationship between Ryan and his mother that brought out the worst in him. She'd seen it too often at family dinners over the years before he'd left. Meredith would say something to needle him—usually comparing him to George—and Ryan would blow up. They'd argue—or, more often, he'd drain his wine glass and head straight out after dinner to the pub, or a club, or somewhere else his mother wouldn't approve of.

Would Ryan be able to hold onto his new, grown-up persona in the face of the one person who'd always, always got under his skin?

That last question distracted Gwen through a lot of the game. She was always torn watching rugby matches anyway, braced for something terrible to happen at the same time as her blood heated and she felt the excitement coursing through her body. And this, from what she could focus on, was a great game. By half-time, even the guy behind her who'd mocked Gwen's words about Ryan seemed to be rethinking his stance—especially after Ryan put the ball over the line for his team's second try.

'I guess he learned some new tricks, playing in France,' the guy said, as he headed to the bar for another pint. 'Might be worth having after all.'

Gwen grinned. If a random stranger could be convinced of Ryan's worth on the pitch, hopefully his parents could be convinced of the same off it.

The second half flew by, as Ryan's team—the Selkies—slipped past their opponents' defence again and again. Evie cheered every time her uncle caught the ball and ran with it, which seemed to be more than anyone else on the pitch. He didn't score any more tries, but, from what Gwen could see, he was instrumental in helping others score them all.

And when, after the final whistle blew, Ryan was dragged onto camera by a TV interviewer, appearing on the large screen, a huge cheer went up through the whole stadium.

'Well!' the interviewer said, as the noise started to abate. 'That was quite a welcome back to Wales, Ryan. How does it feel to be home again?'

He must have known where they were sitting, Gwen realised. Because, as he answered, he looked up directly at them.

'It's great to be back where I belong,' he said, still out of breath from the match. On the screen, Gwen could see sweat dripping down his neck, his dark hair even darker than normal with wetness. His kit was muddy and grass-stained, he had white strapping wrapped around his right thigh, but his smile was jubilant. 'Home with the people I love, especially.'

And in that moment, just for a second, Gwen was sure, so sure, that he was only looking at her.

Ryan ducked out of the interview before the pundit could ask him, inevitably, about George. He wanted to ride this high a bit longer, before the post-game crash hit. His brother would always be a part of his life, his soul—his missing piece now. He'd never had it in him to resent George for being the player, the man, he could never quite be. His big brother had always been his idol, and walking away from playing beside him had been one of the hardest things he'd ever done.

But George was gone, and Ryan needed to think about the future, not the past. *His* future.

Right now, he was on top of the world. He'd proved he deserved the place on the team, had made a great enough showing to put him in serious contention for the national team again, and hopefully to quieten some of the critics who'd been posting on social media, complaining about his signing.

He'd proved to Gwen, he hoped, that he wasn't the same man he'd been when he'd left for France. And that, maybe, he could be part of her family again. An uncle to Evie. A friend to her if she needed it—and somehow he suspected she did.

Most importantly, right now, he hoped he'd made his parents proud of him again. Maybe proud enough to forgive him for the way they'd left things at George's funeral.

He rode that high into the changing rooms, through the throng of celebrating teammates, showering and changing and preparing to celebrate.

'Great game, mate.'

'Good to have you back!'

'Nice to have someone competent at my side again.'

The compliments and back slaps felt good, of course they did. But today was bigger than any game of rugby.

Ryan showered quickly, and shrugged off

requests to join the others down the pub to celebrate.

'Sorry, I need to go find my family,' he told them, hoping his grin didn't give him away too much.

His parents. For the first time in two years he'd see his parents.

And Gwen and Evie. No wonder he was grinning like a mad thing.

Everything was going to be okay.

Gwen had booked them a table for an early dinner at a gastro pub nearby, one that must have sprung up while he'd been overseas but which Gwen seemed familiar with. He'd told her that he'd meet them there, not wanting them to have to hang around at the grounds for him to shower and change. Now it meant that he got to observe them all together, a family, before they realised he had arrived.

They were sitting at a long table in the window, brittle late-March sunshine lighting them up through the glass. He took a moment to watch them, unobserved, and take in the changes—especially in his parents.

They looked older—that was his first thought. Much older than the mere couple of years that had passed should have made them. The sort of older that came with losing a child, he supposed—even if that child had been a grown man.

No one was supposed to outlive their children.

Guilt clutched at his chest, not for the first time, as he thought again that he should have been there for them all. To support them, grieve with them. Even if they hadn't wanted him there.

But despite everything, they looked happy now. He watched as his father made a cloth napkin do tricks for Evie, giving up pennies and sweets when it should have been empty. He'd done the same for him and George. Ryan remembered spending days trying to figure out how the trick was done.

Even his mother looked contented, watching their antics, sipping her wine, and making conversation with Gwen. If he hadn't known her so well, he probably wouldn't have noticed the tension in her shoulders, or the way her gaze darted around the pub anxiously once or twice.

Time to make himself known.

He stepped forward, out of the shadows, and Gwen looked up instantly, as if she were attuned to him.

'Ryan.' She smiled, gentle and soft, and he felt his heart contract at the sight. *Friends*, he reminded himself. *Family.* That was what this was all about. Nothing more.

Then his legs got rugby tackled and, taken by surprise, he actually had to take a step backwards.

'Uncle Ryan!' Evie yelled against his knee-caps. 'You came!'

'Of course I came!' He knelt down to give her a proper hug. 'I said I would, didn't I?'

'Yes, but…' She cast a worried glance back towards her grandmother. 'Nain said not to get my hopes up,' she whispered. 'She said you were…' her nose crinkled up as she tried to find the word '…unreliable.'

'Of course she did,' Ryan muttered. Because he had been. The man he had been would have had a fifty-fifty shot of showing up for this lunch, depending on what other offers he got. His mother wasn't wrong.

But that she'd said it to Evie still hurt. Was Mum even going to give him a chance? Or was her mind made up already?

Well, if it was, it was up to him to change it. That was something else he'd forced himself to learn in France. Grit.

This mattered. So he wouldn't give up. Not ever.

Straightening up to stand again, he took Evie's hand and crossed to the table. Gwen was already standing, and reached over to hug him.

'You were fantastic out there today,' she said, as he resisted the urge to hold her against him for the rest of the day. *Just friends.* 'What an incredible match! The Selkies must be thrilled to have you home again.'

She pulled away, and he felt the loss of her warmth and her support instantly.

'Yeah, I think they're pretty happy,' he said. Then he turned to the other occupants of the table. 'Mum. Dad. It's wonderful to see you. Thanks for coming.'

His mouth was too dry; it was hard to get the words out. He meant it, every word, but he still worried it came out sarcastically or wrong somehow. His parents exchanged a glance, and Ryan felt a squeeze on his hand. Evie, giving him *her* support, even if she didn't really know why he needed it—he was certain Gwen wouldn't have told the little girl the story of his falling out with his family. But she was a perceptive little thing. And she, at least, was happy to have him there. That counted for a lot.

After too long a pause, his father stepped forward. Dylan Phillips was still tall, still more slender than either of his rugby-playing sons had ever been, and still smiling.

'Ryan. It's good to see you, son.' The knot in Ryan's stomach started to loosen as his father reached out to shake his hand, and pat his shoulder. From him, that was an emotional welcome, Ryan knew. One he'd take happily.

'It's good to be home. I missed you all.' He turned to his mother. 'Mum.'

'Ryan.' She nodded her head stiffly, but didn't get up. 'Sit down. You must be hungry after that match, and this place takes for ever to serve the food.'

Ryan allowed himself a small smile as he sat. It might not sound like much, but if his mum was worried about his stomach, that was the first step back to normality. She might make Dad do the cooking, but she had always been concerned about his and George's appetites, and whether they were eating enough to offset all the training and exercise they did. It was one small area in which both brothers had been even in their mother's eyes.

It wasn't much, but he'd take it.

Sitting down, with Evie on one side of him and Gwen on the other, facing his parents on the opposite side of the table, Ryan reached for the menu. His mother was right: as always after a match, Ryan was starving so he ordered the full Sunday roast without hesitation. Evie, he noticed, asked for the same—even when Gwen pointed out she didn't actually like roast beef.

'Maybe I do now,' she said defiantly, and Gwen ordered her the kids' portion.

'And a drink for you, sir?' the waitress asked.

'Just an orange juice, please,' he replied, trying not to feel self-conscious. The other adults all had wine, of course. But he'd worked too hard to backslide into old habits now.

'No beer?' his mother asked, one eyebrow raised. 'Even George would have a pint after a match.'

Ryan shrugged. 'Didn't fancy it.' But Gwen, he realised, was watching him carefully.

Conversation over lunch was stilted, with Gwen desperately trying to keep things flowing. But it was progress. He knew that whenever his mother gave him a certain look she was remembering the funeral—probably remembering the words he'd thrown at her, carelessly, hurtfully and, yes, drunkenly.

'I was never just here on earth to play back-up to my brother! Why couldn't you let me be my own person too? Why is this my fault? I wasn't even there!'

'Exactly,' his mother had replied. *'You*

should *have been there. You left us. And you know that if you'd been there none of this would ever have happened.'*

It had been building ever since the accident, and the funeral had pushed them all over the edge. The worst part was knowing that she was right. On the field and off it, he and George had always looked out for each other. George might have been the one to shine brightest, their golden boy, but he'd needed Ryan there for back-up too. They'd trained together, played together, gone out together… And George had looked out for him too. Making sure he got home after a wild night out—or at least as far as George and Gwen's sofa. Defending him to the coach, and other players, when they'd said Ryan wasn't committed to rugby the way he needed to be. Helping him make sure he was in shape for a game when he'd been slacking off.

George had been his best friend, his whole life. Even when Ryan knew he'd never make it out of his shadow if he stayed.

So he'd left, and George had died. And their mother blamed him.

But now they had to try and come back from that. To build a family again.

'So, how was playing in France different

to playing here in Wales, Ryan?' his father asked casually, as they waited for the food.

Rugby. Common ground, and about as neutral as they were going to get. Ryan jumped on the question and answered at length. One question led to another—about France as a country, the people, the places he'd been.

'And is there anybody special waiting for you over there?' Meredith didn't exactly smile as she asked the question, but it *was* the first she'd asked herself. That counted for something. And apparently meant that Gwen was right—she thought he'd left for a woman.

'No,' Ryan said, carefully not looking at Gwen for fear that his eyes would give too much away. 'I was focussing on my rugby almost entirely. Well, that and learning the language. And a charity I was involved in, helping disadvantaged kids get involved in sport.'

'Really?' Gwen asked. 'Tell me more about that. Maybe there are some ideas we can use at the trust.'

Ryan smiled. Perhaps there was a place for him here, after all. 'What do you want to know?'

After lunch, his parents said their good-byes outside the front of the pub—a stilted hug from his mother and another handshake from his dad. They took Evie off towards the car—with the promise of stopping at the playground on the way—giving him a moment alone with Gwen.

'Thank you,' he said. 'For organising this.'

'I'm sorry.' Gwen sighed. 'I'd hoped your mother would be more...'

'Not like Mum?' he finished for her. Taking her hand in his, he turned her to face him. 'It's okay, Gwen. I know my parents. This was always going to be a long road back. But you've helped me to make a start, and that's all I could have asked for.'

She looked up then, her gaze locking on his and making his heart beat just that little bit faster. 'That's all you wanted from me?'

God, no. He wanted everything. Anything she'd give him. He wanted her close, always. He wanted to hold her at night. He wanted to kiss her, right now...

But she could never know that.

'No.' The denial came out as a hoarse whisper.

'Then what? What else did you come back for, Ryan?'

He couldn't look away from her eyes. In his mind, he imagined swaying closer, an arm around her waist, hauling her against him to kiss her, long and deep and everything…

Everything he couldn't have.

'I want… I want us to be friends again. The way we were before I left. I know… I know I wasn't here when you needed me. When George got hurt, or even after he died. I wasn't here for you or Evie, because I needed to be somewhere else. I needed to go away and become the person you need in your life, as your friend.'

Just friends. That was what he had to focus on. He had to protect himself from the way she made him feel. He could never be George for her, he knew that better than anybody. Even if she wanted him—and he had no evidence that she did—he couldn't let himself fall.

He'd dragged himself out of George's shadow once, made himself the person he wanted to be.

He couldn't risk slipping again now.

'I could… I could really use a friend, as it happens,' Gwen said.

Ryan smiled. 'Then you have one.'

CHAPTER FIVE

GWEN HURRIED ACROSS the road to the playground, praying that Evie and her in-laws hadn't been watching that last interlude between her and Ryan. Although, really, what would they have seen? Nothing had happened. Nothing consequential.

He'd asked for them to be friends again, that was all.

So why did it feel more important than that?

Why had it felt, for just a moment, like he'd been about to kiss her?

She shook her head to banish the thought. It was just those dreams, getting to her. Knowing every night that she'd see Ryan in her sleep. Kissing her. Touching her. Making love to her.

It was driving her insane.

He wanted to be friends, that was all. And that was all she wanted too.

It was absolutely the best thing for both of them.

But that look in his eye…

If they were going to be friends, she needed to get these ridiculous thoughts and dreams about Ryan out of her head. Time to be brutally honest with herself, and face the facts. All the reasons that thinking about Ryan this way was just insane.

Which meant she needed a friend who'd hold her to account and make her do that.

Pulling her phone from her pocket, she texted Joe.

Come over tonight? I need wine and sensible conversation. Just had lunch with Ryan and his parents.

He'd understand enough of the undertones of that without her having to explain—even if she expected that the dream part would come as a bit of a surprise. Unless she'd been far less subtle than she imagined.

Having retrieved Evie from the playground, they waved goodbye to Dylan and Meredith, and Gwen allowed herself to relax just a little. Ryan was right, it was a small first step, but nobody had stormed out, no one had shouted, and everyone had been basically civil. That was all they could have asked for today.

By the time they reached home, it was almost time for Evie's bath and bedtime. Gwen answered the door to Joe as Evie splashed around in her bath, serving bubbly pretend coffee in plastic teacups.

'Come in,' she said. 'You're just in time to help with bedtime stories.'

'As long as you don't want me to do lullabies,' Joe said, handing her a bottle of white wine, already chilled. 'She didn't enjoy my rendition of "Bread of Heaven" last time.'

'I'll do the lullabies, if you pour the wine.'

It took a while to get Evie settled after such an exciting day, and Gwen could hear her daughter telling Joe all about lunch with Uncle Ryan, when she should have been listening to her story. Still, eventually she was asleep, and Gwen could settle down on the sofa with Joe and a glass of that chilled white wine, and try to unpack all her thoughts about the day.

'So, lunch with Ryan and his parents. That must have been interesting.' Joe knew all about the estrangement between Ryan and his parents. Even if he hadn't acted as her confidant the last couple of years, he'd been there at the funeral, right at the end of the week when Ryan and Meredith had let slip the careful control they had all tried to show over the last hours, days, and weeks. When everything they had both not been saying ever since George's accident, or even long before that, had come out in the worst possible way.

'Actually, everyone was surprisingly well behaved.' She remembered how the afternoon had almost ended, and felt the heat flood to her cheeks. 'Well, mostly.' Apart from her imagination.

Joe raised his eyebrows over his wineglass as he took a sip. 'Mostly? Let me guess, Ryan had one too many beers with with meal and said something he shouldn't.'

'Ryan drank orange juice at lunch.' Gwen met Joe's eyes, knowing he'd understand how unusual that was, especially after a match, and one the team had won, as well.

'Because he was trying to impress his parents, or you?' Joe asked, his question right on the nose as usual.

Gwen sighed. 'I wish I knew. Both, maybe? You know, I don't think I've seen him actually drink since he came home. And he's trying so hard with Evie, and with his parents. He didn't start anything with his mother at lunch. Add to that everything he is doing to help me with the trust… He's not the Ryan I remember.'

'And isn't that a good thing?' Joe said. 'Sounds to me like George's little brother has grown up.'

'Maybe. I just can't shake the feeling that…' She trailed off, unable to find the words.

'That he's trying too hard?' Joe guessed.

'That he's trying to be George.' Gwen looked down at her glass, swirling the wine around, watching it cling to the sides. 'There was a moment today when I thought… I honestly thought he was about to kiss me. That's crazy, right? Then he told me he wanted us to be friends again. Like we used to be. Except… everything feels different this time round.'

That made Joe put down his glass on the coffee table and lean forward with interest. 'Okay, now this is getting better. I wondered at you calling me over here just because you'd had lunch with the family. Clearly, you've been holding out on me since Ryan came home. Tell me everything.'

So she did. Hands covering her face for most of it, Gwen recounted everything that had led up to the kiss that wasn't that afternoon—including a rather redacted version of her dreams.

'Hmm.' Joe leaned back against the sofa, his arm flung along the back of the cushions, wearing his thinking face. Gwen knew that face, and knew that her friend wouldn't speak again until he'd marshalled all his thoughts, worked through the options and reached his own conclusions on how best to help her.

So, in the meantime, she topped up their wine glasses.

'The way I see it,' he said, eventually, 'there are three questions here.'

'Only three?' Gwen quipped.

Joe ignored her. 'The first is: did you want him to kiss you and were you disappointed when he didn't? No, don't bother answering that one. I can see from your bright red cheeks that you did. So let's move on to the second: why do you believe that it's a bad thing? Because that's just as obvious from the way you called me over here in a panic.'

Gwen sighed. 'I'd have thought the reasons were obvious too.' Putting down her glass, she ticked them off on her fingers. 'One, I have absolutely no evidence he's even interested in me. It could all be in my head, just my dreams messing with me. He said he wanted to be friends, that's all. Two, he's my brother-in-law. His family would hate the idea of the two of us getting involved. Three, it would be super confusing for Evie. Four, it feels like betraying George, even after everything, and even now he's gone. And five...' She trailed off.

'You think he only wants you to prove he can be as good as George.' Joe completed the thought for her. 'That's what you mean when you said he was trying to be George, right?'

Gwen nodded mutely.

'Hmm,' Joe said, again, unhelpfully.

'You think so too, then?' Gwen asked.

'Oh, hell, no.' Joe flashed her a smile. 'Gwen, the way Ryan looks at you—the way he looked at you when you were still married to his brother, for that matter—I'd never say he only wanted you to prove he could be as good as George. That man adores you, and wants you, don't question that.'

The way he looked at her? *Did* he look at her that way? Anita had said the same thing, but Gwen hadn't let herself believe it.

'But?' There was always a but, wasn't there?

'But that doesn't mean he doesn't *also* want to prove that.'

Gwen slumped back on the sofa. 'I knew I was right.'

'No, listen to me.' Moving closer, Joe put a finger under her chin and forced her to look at him. 'The man wants you. And I reckon you want him too. Otherwise this wouldn't be getting to you this way.'

Biting the inside of her cheek, Gwen searched for words to articulate her feelings, and failed. They were too confusing, there were too many of them, racing around her brain like players on a rugby pitch, all chasing the same ball—her decision on what to do next.

'I… It's like there's something drawing me to him, all the time. I thought it would be awkward, him being back here, after everything that happened with his parents. But I don't think I realised how much I… God, how much I missed just having him here. Just coming around for a cup of tea, or showing up for breakfast. Ryan was the one who always, always listened to me, you know? He *was* my friend, and I *do* want that back. It's just…'

'You're looking at him differently now,' Joe finished for her.

Gwen nodded. She'd assumed it was just his similarity to George, to start with. She had a type, it seemed.

But George…he hadn't been the man she'd fallen in love with, at the end. After Ryan had left, that was when things had started to go really wrong. More arguments. More nights alone. Then the accident, and the brain injury that had turned him into another person altogether…

George had been changed by circumstances beyond his control. Ryan… He wouldn't even need the head injury. All it would take was for him to give up his attempts to mimic his brother's golden ways, and he'd be back to the Ryan she remembered—drinking too much, a new woman every week, taking nothing in life seriously. Everything George had become after his accident.

Gwen couldn't deny that the Ryan who had come home again had changed, for the better. But she knew how easily people could change again. Would Ryan keep up his good behaviour if he didn't get picked for Wales? If he got injured, like George had?

Once he'd proved he could have everything George had, would he stop trying? Or would he even leave again?

She couldn't risk that. Not for herself, and certainly not for Evie.

It was safer to keep things as friends, just like Ryan had said. Especially for her heart.

'I guess you have a decision to make,' Joe said, his expression serious as he looked down at her. 'You need to decide if it's worth the risk to talk to Ryan about this. To see if there's something there between you.'

She met his gaze with her own troubled one. 'I don't see how it can be.'

She just wished that realisation didn't make her heart ache so much.

Two steps forward, one step back, that was how life seemed to Ryan.

Every time he thought he was getting somewhere—bonding with Evie, making small talk with his parents, winning a rugby match, overcoming his primal instincts and agreeing to be friends with Gwen—the universe would do something to knock him back again. Like Gwen cancelling their plans to get together on Sunday.

Well, the universe clearly hadn't been paying enough attention to his form on the rugby pitch, or it would know that the worse the tackle, the more determined he became to get back to his feet and score the next try.

The try, in this case, would be getting Gwen to answer his calls—which she had steadfastly been refusing to do since the text she sent telling him their Sunday plans were off.

Friends answered the phone when friends called, right? Or at least responded to their text messages. Even messaging her about fundraising for the trust hadn't garnered him a response.

She was *definitely* avoiding him. And he needed to know why.

After four days he caved in, and sought advice from the one person who might be able to tell him what was going through Gwen's brain.

'Oh, no.' Joe said, as he exited the studios where he recorded his weekly rugby round-up radio show. Ryan hadn't had his address or his phone number, but finding out when he'd be at the studios had been a very minor piece of detective work—he'd just asked a mate who'd been interviewed on the show the week before. 'I'm not doing this.'

'Doing what?' Ryan asked innocently. 'I just wondered if you'd like to grab a pint, or something. For old times' sake.'

Joe eyed him suspiciously, then sighed. 'Fine. But I thought you were on the wagon.'

Ryan shrugged. 'Let's say I've learned the fine art of moderation.'

That earned a barked laugh from Joe. 'I'll believe it when I see it.'

'That's the idea,' Ryan mumbled.

Joe knew a pub around the corner, so they

headed there. Ryan pulled his wallet out as they approached the bar.

'What're you having?' he asked, as he signalled for the barman's attention.

'Pint of bitter, thanks.'

'Why don't you find us a table?' Ryan suggested, and when he joined Joe at the table a few minutes later he pretended he didn't see the older man's raised eyebrows at the zero per cent label on Ryan's beer bottle.

Joe took a long pull of his pint, then put the glass down. 'So. You want to talk about Gwen.'

'However did you guess?' Ryan asked, dryly.

'Because all *she's* been wanting to talk about this week is *you*.' Joe shook his head. 'I hope you both realise that just because I'm gay it doesn't mean I want to act as your own personal agony aunt.'

'That's not why we turn to you,' Ryan told him.

'Oh?' Joe steepled his fingers as he rested his elbows on the table. 'Enlighten me.'

'We come to you because you've got it all figured out. Life, I mean. You're happy, you're married, you're in love.'

'Gwen had all those things once too,' Joe pointed out.

Ryan held back a wince as he peeled the edge of the label away from his bottle. 'Yeah. But now she's alone again.' And he hated that. Hated seeing her so quiet, clinging to the edges of any crowd, working so hard in the background for the trust but letting others—and especially George's name—take the limelight.

'So you figure you can step into your big brother's shoes for her?' Joe suggested. 'Because I can tell you now, you can't. George was her first love. A one in a million. You can quit drinking, claim you've cleaned up your act, play with her daughter—but you can't be George for her, however hard you pretend.'

What? Ryan looked up, stunned. 'Is that what she truly thinks? That I'm trying to be George?'

'Aren't you?'

'No.' That much he knew for sure. 'I'd never try to replace my brother in her heart. I loved him too, remember.' The words came out hard and sure, and when he met Joe's gaze he tried to put all his belief into it.

After a moment, Joe nodded. 'Okay. So what *are* you doing?'

He knew what he *should* say: that he was trying to rebuild his friendship with Gwen. To be there for her now in a way he hadn't been when she'd needed him most—when George had died. And all of that was true.

It just wasn't the whole story.

Ryan sighed. 'I wish I knew.'

Joe watched him for a moment, then stood up. 'Wait here. This looks like it's going to take a while, and in that case, I need sustenance. You figure out your answers, and I'll be back in a minute.'

While he was gone, Ryan tried to get his thinking straight in his head, but it was hard. So much of the facts and the logic were overruled by his feelings. *George never had that problem.* George had been able to see to the heart of any problem and fix it.

George had never let his heart rule his head, except perhaps when it had come to Gwen.

He wanted them to be friends again. He wanted to be part of the family again. That was the main reason he'd come home, and none of that had changed.

But something else hadn't changed either. He'd thought that his feelings for Gwen, that overwhelming attraction, would have faded while he was away. But it hadn't. And, worse, when he looked at her now, when he met her eye, when she smiled at him…he could almost believe she felt it too.

Before, George would always have been between them. But even now he was dead Ryan knew his brother's shadow was still too long for him to escape. He couldn't be George for Gwen, and he wouldn't be a poor second choice either. Which meant keeping his distance.

However hard that was.

The question was, could he really ever be in Gwen's life and *not* want to be with her? Not want *everything* with her?

Ryan didn't know.

Joe sank heavily back into the chair opposite him. 'Right. I've ordered chips.' He handed Ryan another bottle of alcohol-free beer, and put his own second pint of bitter down on the table. 'Time to talk. Gwen is my friend, and so was your brother. So I'll ask you again. What do you think you're doing?'

As if that wasn't the question he was asking himself every moment these days.

'When I moved to France,' Ryan started, still finding the words even as he talked, 'I was looking for something. A chance to be myself, perhaps, not just George Phillips's younger brother. I wanted out of his shadow, for the first time since we were kids. Since the moment we started playing rugby, in fact. But that wasn't the only reason I left. There was something else I had to get away from here too.'

'Gwen.' Joe shook his head and reached for his pint. 'I knew it. The way you used to look at her…'

'And that's why I left,' Ryan said. 'I had to, before anybody else noticed that. Joe, I loved my brother. I never, for a single moment, actually intended to do anything about my feelings for Gwen. Not even let her know that I had them.'

'I believe you,' Joe said. 'But now you're back and you're starting to think things are different.'

'Aren't they?' Just not as different as Ryan would like.

'Of course,' Joe said with a shrug. 'Gwen's life hasn't been the same since that tackle that took George down. And as much as she's tried to move past it, I'm not really sure she ever has. She is not the same person you knew, Ryan.'

'She is, though. That's half the problem.'

Joe shook his head. 'She's been through too much. You can't just imagine she's going to open her arms and welcome you in, not now. And definitely not you.'

Ouch. That hurt.

'Because I'm George's brother? Or because

she doesn't think she can trust me? I told you, I've changed.' And he'd thought that Gwen believed that too. What had made her doubt him again?

'Honestly? It's probably a bit of both.' Joe gave him apologetic smile, which went no way at all to taking the sting out of his words.

'She doesn't believe I can change.'

'Oh, I don't think that's the problem. Gwen knows better than anybody how people can change. The question is, who have you changed for, and how long can it last?'

Ryan stared at Joe. God, he was sick of being stuck in the past, being forced to play the part he always had. He wanted to move on. Why wouldn't others let him? And most of all, how could he convince Gwen that this was the real him now?

However much he tried to protect his heart from Gwen, her not believing in him would always, always hurt.

Draining his bottle, Ryan got to his feet. 'Thanks, Joe. You've cleared a lot of things up for me.'

'Ryan…' Joe stood up too, but Ryan backed away before he could try and stop him.

'No, I mean it. I'm serious about this— about all of this. About who I am now. About Gwen and being a part of her life—and

Evie's—however she'll have me. About reconciling with my parents. About playing great rugby. These are the things that matter to me, and I'm going to make them happen. I'm done being stuck in the past—being George Phillips's lesser little brother. Being the one who can't settle down, who can't commit, who can't give anybody what they need. I'm done. And I need Gwen to believe that too.'

Otherwise what had it all been for? He'd thought he was ready for this, ready to come home and prove he was a new man. Now he was here, he wasn't sure he was ready at all. But it was too late. He was committed to the tackle, he had to go through with it.

He had to be the man he knew he could be. For Gwen and Evie, and for himself.

'Because you're in love with her.'

'Because she's my friend. This is my family. I lost them all once, and I won't do it again,' Ryan corrected him.

Which meant not giving up.

Slamming his empty bottle down on the table, he walked out, and went to find Gwen.

If anyone had asked—which they hadn't— Gwen would have told them that of course she wasn't avoiding her brother-in-law. He was family. They were friends. Why would she do that?

Evie, the only one who *did* ask after Ryan, mostly wanted to know when her uncle was coming to play again as apparently Monsieur Lapin missed him. Somehow he'd made quite an impact on her. Gwen supposed it was something to do with similar levels of childishness between the pair of them.

But, still, when the knock came on her door on Friday night, her heart skipped a beat. And she knew, without answering it, exactly who'd come to call.

Steeling herself, she took her vegetable stir-fry off the heat, and went to answer the door.

'Ryan.'

'Gwen.'

For a long moment they just looked at each other, and she wondered if his thoughts had strayed the way hers had. Back to her dreams. And back to that moment when they'd almost kissed...

God, he looked good. That dark hair, curling over one brow. Those bright blue eyes, watchful and wanting. Those shoulders, almost filling her doorway.

People talked about how alike the Phillips brothers were but, looking at Ryan now, Gwen could only see the differences. The tiny scar that cut across Ryan's left eyebrow. The way that, although he still stood a head taller than her, the couple of inches he lacked on George's height meant she could stare right up into his eyes. The slightly fuller lips. The even more muscled forearms. The way he wore his polo shirt untucked and with the collar open.

The heat in his eyes that she hadn't seen in George's since even before his accident. She couldn't be imagining that, could she?

Maybe Joe was right. Maybe Ryan really was as tormented by this attraction as she was.

'Can I come in?' His voice rumbled low, and she felt it in her blood. She nodded, and stepped aside to let him enter.

'Are you hungry?' she asked, as she crossed back towards the kitchen. 'I was just making dinner. There's enough for two.' She'd planned on eating it again tomorrow night—cooking for one wasn't interesting enough for her to want to do it more than every other night. Sometimes she and Evie ate together, but Gwen's appetite rarely fancied fish fingers at five p.m.

'Always,' Ryan answered, closer than she'd expected.

She took a breath. 'Great. Come on, then.'

He sat on the stool at her kitchen counter, taking in the surroundings, while she finished off the stir-fry. Sneaking glances at him as she cooked, she saw his gaze linger on Evie's drawings on the fridge, on the school dinner menu pinned to the notice-board, and skip over the large canvas picture of her wedding day by the door.

They managed some small talk while they ate, at least—about how Evie was getting on in reception class, when his next match was and who it was against, how training was going, final figures from the fundraiser and what she had planned next for the trust.

It was only once the dishes were in the dishwasher and they'd moved through to the lounge that Gwen finally found the courage to ask what she really wanted to know.

'Ryan. Why did you come here tonight?'

Lounging against the end of her sofa, too large and too solid in her pretty front room, Ryan gave her a slow smile. 'Would you believe me if I told you I just couldn't keep away?'

Meeting his gaze, she thought, *Yes*. Because she could see the truth there in his eyes.

He was as caught up in this connection between them as she was.

But then he shifted, sitting straighter, and

carried on. 'Truth be told…you were avoiding me, and I figured this was one place you couldn't just run away from. Not with Evie here.'

'So you wanted to corner me? Why?'

'Because I have a proposition for you.'

She suppressed a shiver at the word. 'I'm not sure I like the sound of that.'

'You will.' His voice was firm, certain, and he inched a little closer as he spoke.

Gwen didn't move away as he continued.

'I have an opportunity for you. For the trust, really.'

That…wasn't what she'd been expecting.

'What sort of an opportunity?' she asked, curious. Was he *really* here about the trust? Or was that just an excuse?

'There's a fundraiser coming up for a charity I used to be involved with. The one I told you about at lunch last week? It's kind of a big deal—lots of great contacts there, and I could introduce you to my friends who set the charity up too. I thought we might be able to get some ideas for the trust over here.'

'Sounds fantastic! When is it? And where?' This she was on solid ground with. She and Ryan working together to promote and build the George Phillips Trust, that she could do. They could push aside anything else that was getting between them, complicating matters, and focus on what was really important. This was great.

But Ryan winced. 'That's the only catch. It's over in France, the weekend after next. Do you think Evie would be okay with my parents for a couple of nights?'

A couple of nights. That meant she'd be with Ryan, abroad, in some hotel or another, for two nights. Trying not to think about kissing him. Or dream about him naked.

Oh, there were so many ways that this could go wrong.

But it was for the trust...

'I'll ask them,' Gwen said, and hoped she wouldn't regret it later.

CHAPTER SIX

RYAN COLLECTED GWEN from his parents' house the next Friday morning. It felt strange, pulling up outside their driveway, seeing the house—not the one where he'd grown up, but the one he had helped to move them into after George had bought it for them.

He didn't want to push his luck, so he lingered in the hallway while Gwen said her goodbyes. Her bag was already in the car, ready to go. As she ran through Evie's routine one last time with his mother, Ryan looked around him at the frames on the wall. His parents' wedding day, George and Gwen's wedding day, plenty of photos of Evie, even more of George, mostly wearing his Wales kit. But not one of him. He wasn't even surprised.

'Okay,' Gwen said. 'Are we ready?'

'When you are.' Half of him still believed she was going to pull out at the last second. That he couldn't truly be so lucky as to get a second chance with this woman, even as friends. That, one way or another, he was going to hell for this. Coveting his brother's wife, even after that brother was dead.

Evie tackled his knees again and he crouched down to hug her. 'So, are you going to be in charge of your grandparents while your mum is away?' Evie laughed. 'I'm serious! Who knows what kind of trouble they'd get into without you here to look after them?'

'I think we'll all muddle along quite nicely together,' his father said, coming to pick Evie up and rest her against his hip. 'You two just relax and enjoy yourselves. It's been a long time since Gwen had a holiday.' He gave Ryan a pointed look, a look Ryan knew meant that he was on its way to having his father's approval—as long as he could make Gwen happy.

Good thing that was just exactly what he intended.

'It's not a holiday, Dylan,' Gwen said, picking up her bag. 'It's work. For the trust.'

'Of course it is, love,' his father replied mildly. Ryan wondered exactly what sort of a trip he really thought this was, but he didn't dare ask.

Or hope.

With one last hug and a kiss from Evie,

Ryan guided Gwen into the car, and drove them towards the station. She was quiet this morning, but he supposed that was to be expected. This was new territory for both of them.

He just hoped it gave them more than a few good contacts for the trust.

By the time they reached the Eurostar at King's Cross, Ryan thought he might have just about convinced Gwen that this was a good idea again. She'd changed her mind halfway to London, but by then it had been too late to turn back and she'd known it.

'I know I'm being silly,' she said as they took their seats on the train. 'I've just never been a different country from my daughter before.'

Ryan winced. He hadn't thought about it like that. Obviously there was a steep learning curve involved if he really wanted to be part of this family. 'Honestly? Where we are going could be closer than you would have been if I'd taken you to Scotland.'

Gwen laughed. 'I suppose so. Like I said, I'm being silly.'

'No.' Ryan reached across the table between them to take her hand. 'You're being a mum.'

The train pulled away from the station, and they both sat and watched the city passing by, becoming countryside.

'What made you pick France?' Gwen asked, apropos of nothing.

'Uh…' He'd expected to have this conversation at some point over the next couple of days. Just not quite yet. His motives for moving to France had been so tied up with the woman opposite him, it was hard to even discuss it without confessing the secret he'd held so long in his heart.

'I mean, wouldn't it have been easier to stay in the country at least?' Gwen went on. 'I'm sure there were English teams desperate for you to move to them. Why France?'

Relief surged through him. This was about practicalities, not the emotional side of his decision. That he could answer.

'I guess I figured that if I was going to make the move, it might as well be a big one.' Ryan shrugged. 'Growing up, training was such a huge part of our lives it didn't leave a lot of time for anything else. School holidays were just an opportunity to train more. Travel, holidays—they weren't really on the cards for us. You must know that from George. Anyway, I guess I figured if I was going to leave Wales I might as well go somewhere completely different. And they play some great rugby over there.' Getting better at his sport, more serious about it, had been a big part of his decision too.

'Did you like France, then?' Gwen asked.

'More than I thought I would even,' Ryan said with a smile. 'Nowhere will ever beat Wales for beauty, friendliness, and just feeling like home. But France gave me something else. Something I don't think I even knew I needed until I got there.'

They sat back as the train continued its journey, ducking down into the tunnel under the Channel, leaving rain-splattered England behind. The silence between them was comfortable, companionable, the way it always had been with the two of them.

After a while, Gwen turned back to him. 'Can I ask where we'll be staying?' She took a sip of the coffee she'd ordered. 'I mean, is it a hotel, are we by the beach…?'

The next, slightly awkward point. 'Actually, we're going to stay at my house.'

Gwen's eyebrows shot up over her coffee cup. 'You bought a house? And you kept it, even though you moved home?'

He knew it wasn't what she'd have expected from him, but he hoped it was just further proof of the man he was now. Not the

Ryan who'd spent all his sponsorship money on cars and in bars, while George had been buying their parents a house.

These days he owned property. He had an investment plan, a pension, an actual financial advisor.

'Yeah. Buying it wasn't exactly in the grand plan when I moved over there. But, trust me, you'll understand when you see the house.'

She looked intrigued now. Good. He'd given her something else to focus on, other than leaving Evie behind, and the idea of it being just the two of them in his home for the next two days.

Even if he knew that was definitely all he was going to be thinking about, at least until they arrived.

'Okay, that is not a house.' Gwen stared up at the building Ryan had brought her to. She'd been expecting some sort of townhouse or apartment, perhaps a tumbledown holiday cottage at best. But this place, Ryan's home…

It blew her away. Despite the sign at the end of the driveway saying 'Le Manoir', it looked more like an ancient castle than a manor house. The sort where fairy tales might come true. It even had a turret, for heaven's sake. The front door was made of heavy oak, and the windows were mostly arches carved out of the stone. Apart from the extension, that was. It was off to the side of the older house, a glass and wood extension, tied into the original structure by the huge glass windows that filled must what must've once been a high arched passageway for horses, perhaps.

'That's where the swimming pool is,' Ryan told her. He looked amused at her open-mouthed reaction.

'Of course you have a swimming pool,' she muttered.

'It's good for my muscles after a game.' Ryan grabbed her hand, holding her suitcase with the other. 'Come on, let me show you around inside.'

The inside was no less impressive than the exterior. A large modern kitchen led to a dining hall with the sort of long wooden table Gwen could imagine being used for banquets. The living space featured large comfortable sofas that fitted perfectly in the oversized room. It was the fireplace that caught Gwen's attention, though. It was late spring, and warmer here than at home. They would probably have no need to light it while she was there. But just looking at it reminded her of all the dreams that Ryan had featured in recently.

Fighting a blush, she turned her back to it. 'Upstairs?' Then, at Ryan's smirk, she realised the connotation of her request, and the heat hit her cheeks with full force.

'Absolutely,' Ryan said, turning to lead her towards the stairs.

The stairs were the first thing about Ryan's *manoir* that she didn't actually like. As she climbed them gingerly, Ryan tried to reassure her.

'I mean, the staircase has lasted four hundred years—I don't reckon it's about to give way now. And, actually, spirals are a very secure shape for a staircase.'

Gwen looked through the gaps between the steps, and felt the uneven surfaces of the wood under her feet, the oak so hard it had almost petrified into rock, and shuddered. Instead, she focussed on Ryan's broad back as they climbed. As distractions went, it was one of the more pleasant ones she could think of.

'I thought you might like this room,' he said, motioning to one of the doorways as they reached the landing at last.

'I'm sure it'll be fine,' Gwen said, secretly slightly relieved that he hadn't picked her a room up the next flight of stairs.

Then he pushed the door open, and she saw inside. 'Oh. Wow.'

The bedroom was huge, probably as big as the first flat she and George had shared together in Cardiff. It had windows on two walls, looking out over the extensive grounds surrounding Le Manoir. The floor was stone, smoothed by the ages, and covered with warm, fluffy rugs. Another fireplace took up a large portion of wall here, with a sheepskin rug on the floor in front of it, just as she'd imagined in her dreams. But turning away from that didn't help, because it only led her to look at the other focal point of the room—a giant four-poster bed, laden with blankets and cushions and a satin eiderdown.

'Do you like it?' Ryan asked, sounding concerned. 'There's an en suite bathroom through that door just there. And it shouldn't get too cold at night now, but if it does I can always light the fire. If you don't like it—'

'I love it,' Gwen admitted. 'It's…like something from a dream.' A filthy dream. One she'd been trying to pretend she wasn't still having every single night.

Ryan's smile relaxed. 'Great. Do you want to see the other bedrooms? You might see one you prefer.' But he left her suitcase by the bed before they headed back out to explore the other rooms. It was clear he'd chosen this one for her, and Gwen thought he'd chosen well.

'How many bedrooms are there?' she asked, after they'd inspected the other two bedrooms on the same floor—one another double, one a twin—and he was leading her up another terrifying spiral staircase to the top floor.

'Five, in total,' he replied. 'There's two more up here. Mine and, well, another.'

She was surprised, and grateful, that he hadn't put her in the room next to his—if only because it saved her from having to climb that second staircase. Not to mention that putting temptation a little further out of her grasp seemed like a good idea.

But when he opened the door to that second bedroom, she saw why instantly.

It was a child's room. Oh, it was neutral enough—a simple wooden bed with fresh cotton sheets and a small dressing table or desk and a stool. The walls were painted a light cream rather than left as exposed stone like most of the house. The pale curtains fluttered in a slight breeze, and Gwen crossed to the window to look out over a meadow of wildflowers. She turned back to take in the rest of the room: the toy chest by the antique wardrobe; the small collection of soft toys on the pillow—including another Monsieur Lapin, or perhaps Mademoiselle Lapin since this one was wearing a pink tutu.

Most telling, though, was the print that hung over the desk. In elaborate fonts, it read *'Though she be but little, she is fierce.'*

'Shakespeare?' Gwen asked, pointing to it.

Ryan shrugged sheepishly. 'It seemed appropriate. I mean, she's the daughter of a rugby legend. She's hardly going to let herself be pushed around, is she? Especially not with you as her mother.'

Stunned, Gwen spun to face him. 'You made this room for *Evie*?'

'How many other little girls do you think I know?' Ryan asked, with a laugh. Then he must have seen her troubled expression, because he crossed the room to her and grabbed her hands. 'Gwen. Whatever you're thinking, stop. I had this room decorated ages ago—not long after George's accident, actually. I figured that the three of you…well, I knew things would be more difficult for you all. So I figured that maybe you might all want to get away from things at home for a while sometime. I'd thought that you might all come and stay one day. You and George were to have the master suite next door, and Evie could stay here.'

He'd been planning on making amends with George, with all of them, for a while, then. That was good to know. Except…

'And where would you have been?' Gwen asked, looking up into those bright blue eyes. So like George's, and yet not.

Ryan couldn't have known how truly terrible things had been for them after the accident. In fact, she'd made sure that he hadn't. But all the same he'd planned this place as a getaway for them if they'd needed it—as much as a getaway for himself. But what had he been escaping from?

Ryan just shrugged again, and turned away towards the door. 'I think that would have depended on whether you and George wanted me around. I'd hoped...well, it doesn't matter now.'

'That you two could have been friends again?' Gwen guessed.

Ryan nodded. 'I... I hate that he died, not having forgiven me for moving away. For not being on the pitch that day he was hit. Even after his accident, I left before he was properly awake. Our last conversation was that argument before I moved to France.'

Biting the inside of her cheek, Gwen desperately tried to control all the emotions surging through her. She wanted to say something—anything that could make this all better. But how could she?

The truth was, George never *had* forgiven

his brother before he died. It was another bit-
terness that had soured his last years. But
another truth was that, if he had been himself after that accident, she liked to hope he
would have done, long before his death. Because the George she'd married hadn't held
a grudge, although the George he'd become,
especially after his accident, might well have
done. But how could she explain that to Ryan
without tarnishing his memory of his golden
brother for ever?

Not to mention that if Ryan knew the truth,
that was one more person in on the secret she
was desperate to keep. And there were already too many people who knew for her to
be comfortable risking one more.

So instead she rested a hand against his
arm, her head against his shoulder, and whispered, 'I know.'

She did. All the ugly words she and George
had thrown at each other those last months.
Every time she'd been unable to keep her tem-
per, even though she'd *known* it wasn't her
husband speaking but the injury.

They'd become one and the same, in the
end.

There'd been no love left there at all, and
that had eaten away at the inside of her for too
long now. She'd hate Ryan to feel that too. To

know that his brother had died hating him—
because he'd hated everything by the end.

'Come on. Show me this bachelor pad master suite, then.' She flashed him a smile, and
he returned it, although his never reached his
eyes. Probably hers didn't either.

But he shook off his mood, all the same.
For her.

'Okay. And then, if you're not too scared to
make it down the stairs, I'll make you dinner.'

Dinner was simple—pasta with chicken and
sauce, from the hamper he'd ordered to be
delivered prior to their arrival, served with
a good white wine he even allowed himself
half a glass of—but Gwen seemed to enjoy
it. Well, mostly she just seemed amazed at
the idea of him cooking at all, and by the
house.

Good. That meant he was defying her ex-
pectations. Proving she wasn't the man she
thought he was.

And that was why he'd brought her there.
Well, that and the fundraiser tomorrow night.

He had to keep his focus on that. They
were here for work. Otherwise it would be far
too easy to let himself believe that Gwen had
come to France purely because she wanted to
spend time with him.

'Keep your head on straight, Ryan.' That was what his friend Julienne had used to say to him whenever he had got distracted in training or worked up on the pitch.

And it was what he needed to do now. Keep his head on straight and protect his heart.

After dinner they retired to the living room, glasses in hand—although he'd switched to water, and talked some more. Outside, the sun was sinking, the sky fading from blue to orange, to pink, to navy, all the way to black.

'It's beautiful here,' Gwen said, perched on the window seat as she stared out at the night. 'And the stars! I don't think I've ever seen so many of them. Not even in the valleys back home.'

'It's one of the things I loved most about this place when I bought it.' Ryan moved from the sofa to sit on the other end of the window seat, just to be close to her. God, he had it bad. 'You can sit here and feel like you're the only person around for miles.'

That made her shift her attention from the sky to him. 'You see, that surprises me. Back home, you always wanted to be where the people were.'

He shrugged. 'Like I said, I changed.'

'Yes…but you didn't tell me why.' Wrapping her arms around her knees, she tilted her head to the side as she watched him. 'Will you? Now?'

Why he'd changed? As if it was a decision he'd made one day, rather than something that had just sort of happened to him.

'I... I moved to France to get out of George's shadow, in large part. To find out who I could be if I wasn't George Phillips's younger brother.' His brother's name still felt heavy in his mouth after all this time. 'It wasn't because I resented him, or didn't love him. I just... I needed to know. Does that make sense?'

Gwen's smile was gentle. 'It does. George was...well, his reputation, his presence could be overwhelming at times.'

She must have felt it too, he realised. She'd spent most of her adult life as 'George Phillips's wife'. An appendage to his greatness. Supporting him, loving him—but what had she given up to do so? What dreams had she had before it had become clear that being George's wife was a full-time job in itself?

Not now, though. Now she was forging her own path with the trust—even if she was still hiding behind his name, to a degree. She was doing the work because she believed in it, and she was doing it well.

Ryan's heart ached with pride for her. And

the realisation that she really was the only other person in the world who could understand exactly how he'd felt.

'When I got here, I didn't know anybody, and my schoolboy French was pretty lousy at the best of times. That first night, sleeping in some motel room near the training grounds, alone, with a dog barking outside keeping me awake—although my own nerves were doing that anyway—I started wondering if I'd made a mistake. George, my parents, even my agent—not to mention the managers of Welsh rugby—had tried to convince me to stay in Wales, to get more caps for my country before I looked overseas. So I was lying there, thinking that they were probably right.'

'What changed your mind?' Gwen asked. 'I mean, I assume if you'd kept thinking that way you'd have come home before now.'

'Yeah.' Ryan tipped his head back against the wall behind him, remembering the horrors of his first day at training. Sleep-deprived, slow, and unable to understand half of his teammates—unless they wanted him to—he'd struggled. 'It was hard, to start with. Then after the first week or so I figured... I chose this. I made this decision. And even if I hadn't, it was what I had. So now I had to figure out a way to make it work.'

'And you did.'

'And I did.' She was still watching him, studying him, and Ryan smiled a self-deprecating smile to try and distract her. 'It was just little things to start with. Making an effort to talk to a new teammate every day, doing extra training with them when I could. Working on my French in the evenings rather than going out to the pub. The language barrier meant I really had to listen when the team were discussing strategies and plays—even though everyone's English was far better than my French.

'Suddenly I was more focussed and more sober than ever before. And my rugby started to improve. A lot. So I kept going. Until one day I woke up and realised I wasn't the same person who'd moved here. I wasn't thinking about myself in comparison to George any longer. I was just me—and I liked the person I'd become.'

'I like him too,' Gwen whispered.

He couldn't look away from her eyes. Not when, for the first time, he saw everything he'd ever hoped or dreamed he might see there in the depths of them.

Possibility. The smallest chance that she might feel the same way about him as he did about her. As he'd been feeling for so long now.

He wanted to kiss her, the desire and the need to welling up in him until it was almost impossible to think about anything else. But then, all of a sudden, Gwen jumped up from the window seat and held out a hand to him.

'Come on,' she said. 'I want to go swimming.'

The swimming pool was one of the few things he had added to the original building, and something he'd never regretted for a moment. Built inside what had originally been a courtyard used to bring horses and carriages through to the stables behind Le Manoir, it benefited from stone walls on two sides, huge archways now covered with glass on the other two and, his favourite feature, a glass roof.

Watching Gwen float on her back in the moonlit water, staring up at the stars overhead, Ryan knew this was exactly why he'd brought her here. She looked so relaxed, her arms stretched out to the sides, her caramel hair darkened into a halo around her head. Apart from the occasional lazy kick of her feet to keep herself afloat, she was entirely at peace.

Ryan lowered himself into the water, grateful that the pool was heated, and pushed off from the side towards her. The pool wasn't huge, but it was certainly big enough for two.

'This is so beautiful,' Gwen said, lowering her legs until she was upright again. She swept her damp hair back, away from her face, and smiled at him. 'How did you ever manage to leave here and come home to Wales?'

He looked at her, standing waist deep in the water, her plain navy swimsuit clinging to every one of her curves, her skin shimmering with water droplets in the moonlight. And he couldn't not say it. Couldn't hide from her a moment longer. Not in this place, at this moment.

'There were even more beautiful sights back home,' he told her, knowing his eyes would leave her in no doubt exactly which sights he was talking about.

'Ryan…'

He stepped closer, until he could place one hand at the curve of her waist. She didn't back away.

'Gwen, you know why I brought you here—to help you with the trust. But also because… I wanted to show you this place. Show you completely who I became here.'

'I know.'

She was so close now he'd barely have to

move to kiss her. To have her whole body pressed against his, exactly how he wanted it.

But he couldn't. Not without saying something more.

'But there was another reason too,' he went on. 'I brought you here because I'm selfish, and however much I know there can't be anything between us, I just wanted to spend this time with you, the two of us. Alone.'

'Why?' she asked, looking up at him, her eyes serious in the moonlight. 'What did you hope we could do here we couldn't do at home?'

Oh, she was killing him. There was knowledge in her eyes. And she was standing close enough to him that she had to be able to *feel* exactly what he wanted, almost.

But she was going to make him say it.

Fine. Then he was going to say it all.

'Gwen. You have to know by now how much I want you. How goddamn tempted I am by you every second we're together. And I don't know if you feel the same way—'

She gave a low, throaty chuckle at that. 'Don't you? Ryan...ever since you came back... I've been *dreaming* of you. Of us. Imagining what it could be like...'

That knowledge sent all the blood in his body directly to one place, which was no help at all in figuring out what the hell to say next. She dreamed of him. She *wanted* him.

'This might be the worst idea in the world…' He leaned in closer, until his lips were almost brushing hers. 'But I really, really need to kiss you right now.'

He waited, just millimetres away. He needed it to be her choice. For her, and for him.

He needed to know he truly wasn't alone in this. Not any more.

The moment that followed seemed to last for ever. Above the stars carried on twinkling, around them the night grew only darker. He could feel her breath against his mouth, the thump of her heart in her chest, too rapid for her to pretend this wasn't affecting her at all.

And then, just when he was about to give up hope, Gwen let out a small, breathy sound of surrender and, stretching up on tiptoe, she wrapped one hand around the back of his neck and dragged his mouth to hers.

Ryan felt the kiss in every cell of his body. He reached around, lifting her until her long bare legs wrapped around his waist. God, she was so hot against him, so soft, so everything he'd dreamed of. Her mouth never left his, and he never wanted it to.

He wanted to take her, here, now, just like this. Wanted to sink into her and stay there until the unbearable longing he'd felt for her for so long was assuaged—at least for now.

And from her kiss, her touch, she wanted it too. At least, her body did.

But Ryan wanted more than just her body. He knew that now.

He'd tried to pretend that what he felt for Gwen was purely physical, that moving away would remove the torment of wanting something he couldn't have. But it had never stopped him thinking about her.

Because this wasn't lust. It was love.

For him, anyway.

And maybe it never would be for her. But he needed it to be something more than a passion-filled moment she'd regret in the morning.

He wanted *so* much more than that.

Gently, reluctantly, he sat her on the side of the pool, drawing away from the kiss with slow, exquisitely painful movements. Gwen followed him, pressing light, teasing kisses against his lips until he thought he'd give in entirely—or they'd both fall back into the pool.

'Gwen. Sweetheart, we have to stop.' God, how he hated saying those words.

'What?' Her eyes were dazed with lust, and Ryan couldn't help but smile at the sight. 'Why?'

'Because… I won't rush into this. If we're going to do this at all, I need to know it's something more than just one night. One incredible, mind-blowing night.'

He swayed forward and kissed her again. He knew it would be—both incredible and mind-blowing.

Which also meant it was worth waiting for.

'You're right.' Gwen pulled away, but not before kissing him back. 'There's too much at stake here. Evie, your family, the trust…'

'Yeah.' And more than any of that, Ryan needed to know that he meant more to her than just a stand-in for George. That she wanted the man he was now. And that meant showing her all of him.

Starting with the fundraiser tomorrow night. He needed to show her his life in France. To prove to her that this change wasn't just for a season, or for a chance to play rugby in Wales.

It was who he was now. And he hoped that man might be someone she could love.

They stayed, foreheads resting against each other, her sitting on the edge of the pool, him waist deep in the water and willing his body to calm down and behave, both of them breathing too heavily to pretend this was anything other than torture. And all the time, that hope battered at the bars he'd put around his heart to stop her getting in, back when she had still been his brother's wife.

He wasn't ready to believe, just yet, that she could really be his.

'Are you okay getting back to your room?' he asked, and Gwen nodded.

Pulling up her legs, she got to her feet and padded over to where he'd left a stack of fluffy towels for them. 'I'll see you in the morning?' she asked, looking back over her shoulder.

'I'll make you breakfast,' he promised.

Ryan watched her go, through the doors back into Le Manoir proper. Then he swallowed, pushed off from the side, and forced himself to swim a few lengths.

There was no way he was sleeping tonight without *some* sort of exertion. Even if it wasn't the one he desperately wanted.

CHAPTER SEVEN

GWEN WOKE UP still dreaming of that kiss.

For a moment she lay starfished in her four-poster bed, trying to untangle what had really happened from the dreams that had kept her tossing and turning all night. In the end, she decided that the ratio of dream to reality was far too weighted on the dream side. She'd need to do something to correct that…

Except Ryan was right. This wasn't something that could be rushed into. This attraction between them was so new, so unexpected, she couldn't just jump in without considering all the options. Without remembering all the reasons she shouldn't jump at all.

But on the other hand…this wasn't going away. Not her dreams, not the chemistry between them. In fact, she was willing to bet that now she knew for sure he wanted this too, the pull towards him was only going to get worse.

While she'd been able to tell herself that this was just one-sided, that it was a misplaced attraction based on him fulfilling her obvious type, and the fact that she'd missed him and his support while he'd been away, she'd still had a chance at keeping things between them friends only.

Now…she knew, in her gut, it was only a matter of time before she gave in. To the dreams, the chemistry, the pull…to everything she wanted.

She just needed to get it all straight in her head first. They had another couple of days here in France. She needed to use that time wisely, to figure out what she wanted from Ryan. Because it was clear that just one night, to get rid of these dreams, wasn't on offer. Ryan had always been an all or nothing sort of man.

And now she was pretty sure he wanted everything. She just wasn't sure she could give it, not while keeping her own secrets.

Not to mention that the idea of giving everything of herself again, after George had thrown it all back in her face at the end, was kind of terrifying.

God, the whole thing was a mess. But perhaps, for now, she could just take it one step at a time. Starting with breakfast.

Forcing herself from the comfort of the bed, Gwen showered and dressed, and headed downstairs in search of the food she'd been promised.

Ryan was already up, flipping through a pile of post that had obviously arrived for him while he'd been gone, the coffee-maker bubbling away behind him.

'Apparently I screwed up the mail redirection,' he said, motioning to the pile of post. 'But the coffee is brewing and I have the oven warming for pastries. *Pain au chocolat, pain au raisins*, croissants, or all three?'

Gwen grinned. 'All three, please.'

'An excellent choice.'

He got up from his stool and headed for the stack of bakery bags on the counter, pausing on the way to press a kiss to the very corner of her mouth. Gwen resisted the urge to turn her head and make the kiss something deeper—but only just.

Really, with her body and her subconscious betraying her like this, how was her mind supposed to keep them in check until she'd had a chance to fully decide how she wanted to proceed?

To distract herself from more kissing thoughts, she picked up her phone and tapped out a quick good-morning message to Evie, via her grandmother's phone. She'd call later, after breakfast.

Then she scrolled through her emails and spotted one from Joe. She frowned. That was unusual; he normally texted or even called. But when she opened it, she saw why. He'd forwarded her a link to an online news and gossip magazine featuring a full-size photo of her and Ryan, standing together at the trust fundraiser the previous month.

'Looks like you can't keep out of the British papers, even when you *are* on your best behaviour,' she joked, holding the screen up for him to see. Ryan just rolled his eyes.

Amused, and a little distracted by quite how much like a couple they looked through the photographer's lens, Gwen started to read out the copy that went with the image.

'"Wild boy of rugby Ryan Phillips is back in the country—and stepping out with a new woman on his arm! Only this time it's his sister-in-law, Gwen Phillips, tragic widow of the late George. The pair was attending a fundraiser for the George Phillips Trust, raising money for people who suffer life-changing brain injuries. But we couldn't help but notice just how *happy* the two of them seemed to be together…"'

Trailing off, Gwen looked again at the

photo. In it, she was looking up at Ryan, laughing as he smiled down at her. Their gazes were locked on each other, she realised. Like there was no one else in the room.

No wonder they hadn't seen the photographer.

'It was a fun night,' Ryan said, nonchalantly, as he put the baking tray of pastries in the oven. 'Of course we were having a good time.'

Gwen turned back to the article. '"Speaking to an old friend and teammate of Ryan's, we heard that the lovable rogue—"' Ryan snorted at that '"—might have been carrying a flame for his brother's wife for longer than we thought. 'Ryan always fancied Gwen,' our source told us. 'But she only ever had eyes for George.'"' She put the paper down. 'Well, that bit's rubbish, anyway.'

Except Ryan had gone very still over by the oven.

'I wonder who gave them that quote.'

His voice sounded strange too.

'Ryan?' Gwen stared at him. 'They just made it up, right? Nothing to worry about.'

Except Ryan just sighed and slowly turned around. 'I don't know who said it,' he told her. 'But I'm not entirely surprised that someone did. Even Joe told me it was obvious—that I, well, was attracted to you.'

'But now, right? Not back then.' How could he have? She'd been George's wife.

The idea that he could have been wanting her all those years ago…it made her stomach feel uneasy. Apart from that night they'd met, in the bar, he'd never even given her a *hint* that he'd found her attractive, let alone anything else.

But he wouldn't have, would he? Because she had been with George. And whatever anyone might say about Ryan's morals—and they did—he would never had done anything to hurt his brother. She knew that.

Crossing to the counter where she sat, he laid his palms flat on the surface, leaning across to look her in the eyes. A soft smile lingered around the corners of his mouth. 'Gwen, I've never been able to look at you and not want you. Not since that first night I met you in that bar.'

His words caught her in the solar plexus. In an instant her whole history unravelled and re-formed from that night, except this time it was Ryan who took her number at closing time. Ryan who called and asked her out. Ryan she fell in love with, not George.

How different might her life have been if things had happened that way?

'The number of times I cursed myself for a

damn idiot for leaving you for a second that night. For giving George the chance to sweep in and charm you.' He shook his head, his smile rueful. 'But in the end I figure that the past is the one thing you can't change. And, in truth, I wouldn't even want to.'

'You wouldn't?' she asked quietly. But in her head the reasons were already falling into place.

Ryan had been a hot mess back then. Reckless, unreliable, and definitely not one for settling down. At best, they'd have had a couple of nights together before he'd moved on. And then she might never have met George. And no matter how horribly it had all ended, she'd never have wanted that. They had been happy, for a time. And more than that...

If she'd never met George that night, she'd never have had Evie. And that was unthinkable.

'I wasn't the right person for you back then,' Ryan said, echoing her thoughts. 'Maybe I could have been—God knows you'd have been worth changing for. But given my track record, odds are good I'd have screwed it up somehow. And besides...'

He trailed off, and Gwen found herself leaning closer. She needed to hear this, however hard it was. 'What?'

'George loved you so much. And you loved him. I'd never want to deny either of you that.' He looked away. 'Especially given how short the time you had together was.'

Of course he wouldn't. He wasn't that kind of man. Which only made her like him more.

But it also brought another, horrible thought to the front of her mind.

He'd said he was attracted to her. That he wanted her. But after last night in the pool, the things he'd said then…she wondered if it was more. How hard it had been for him to watch her and George together if he wanted more from her than just a night in her bed.

'I need to know it's something more than just one night,' he'd said. How much more?

She needed to know the truth. 'Be honest with me. Was that…? I mean, was *I* the reason why you left Wales?'

'One of the reasons,' Ryan admitted. 'I'd never have done anything about it, you understand. I never even wanted you to know. George was my brother, and I loved him. I'd never do anything to hurt him, you know that. But that couldn't change how I felt about you.'

'Lust,' she said, giving him one last way out of this. 'That's what you felt.'

His gaze was almost pitying. 'I tried to tell myself that too. It was just my body making demands. Just a crush even. Wanting what my brother had, perhaps. I figured that moving miles away, with a whole new nation of women for me to flirt with, would solve the problem.'

'And did it?'

'Not for a second.'

Gwen gasped in a huge lungful of air. 'Am I…? Am I why you came back? Did you have this planned from the start?'

Ryan shook his head. 'No. No, Gwen…' He swerved around the counter to her side and picked up one of her hands, holding it close to his chest. 'I came home for all the reasons I told you. I never lied about that. I wanted to play rugby for Wales again. I wanted to make up with my parents, if that's even possible. But more than anything I needed… I needed a family again—you and Evie. But I only ever imagined it could be as Uncle Ryan, nothing more. Not until…'

'Until?'

'Until that night at the fundraiser. When you looked up at me like you're doing in that photo. And I saw something in your eyes that gave me…hope, I guess.'

'I'd been dreaming about you.' Ryan's smile spread across his face until it could only be classified as a smug grin.

'You said that last night, and I was too busy kissing you to ask you to elaborate. So, tell me more about this…'

'No.' Gwen knew she was blushing; her cheeks felt fiery hot. 'I just… Before you left, I'd never thought of you that way. Not after that night we met, when you were just some good-looking stranger. From that day on, you were George's brother. And I loved you as family, but it never even occurred to me…'

'Of course it didn't,' Ryan said easily. 'I never imagined it would. You loved George with everything that you were. Nothing that happens now that he's gone will ever change that.'

She *had* loved George. Until he'd become someone she hadn't even recognised.

'But since you came back…' She risked looking up, and found nothing but understanding in his eyes. Well, understanding and an underlying core of heat. Want. One that she knew was echoed in her own gaze. 'I *see* you. All of you.'

'That's all I ever wanted.'

It wasn't exactly how Ryan had intended to confess to Gwen that he'd been crazy about her for years, but actually it hadn't worked out too badly. He hadn't said the L word, at least. That would be far too much, too fast, too soon. And besides, Ryan wasn't sure he really knew what love looked like—except that he'd known it when he'd seen it between Gwen and George. *They* weren't there yet, however fast he could feel his own heart hurtling towards it.

He'd always known that if he let himself feel, let himself fall, he'd be head over heels for Gwen in seconds flat. That was one of the reasons he'd held back, the moment he'd seen her smiling at his brother at that bar, as Ryan had downed another shot he didn't need. From that moment, seeing how happy she made George, he'd vowed to put as much distance as he could between them. Wanting his brother's wife was bad enough. Loving her? That would be unbearable. Especially when he knew she didn't even see him.

Still, as he held her gaze and basked in the warmth of it, he knew she wasn't entirely comfortable with this new revelation just yet. He'd told her last night he'd wait until she was ready for this to mean something more than just one night, but he hadn't admitted how much more he really wanted. He thought she knew now. And it made sense that it would take her a little time to adjust to it.

So he'd give her that time, and change the subject.

Flicking through the pile of post that had arrived while he'd been away in Wales, he pulled out the one he was looking for. Thick, creamy card stock with scrolling gold text, laid over the image of the Château des Ducs de Bretagne in Nantes. An invitation…one he might well have refused if it hadn't given him the opportunity to take Gwen.

He'd responded to the email invite from Julienne, but it seemed he'd been sent the real thing, as well. He handed it to Gwen.

'If that photo hasn't put you off fundraisers and me for life, this is the event we're going to tonight.' He handed over the invitation, and let her take it in.

'At the Château des Ducs de Bretagne?' Gwen's brow creased in concentration as she tried to translate the French on the invitation. 'That sounds a lot fancier than the local chain hotel I was expecting. I'm rather out of practice at the high society thing, and I'm really not sure I packed for an actual castle.'

The oven beeped, and he removed the pastries, placing one of each on a plate and handing it to her.

'It's not *actually* a duke's castle any more,' Ryan explained. 'It's basically a museum. Think of it like Caerphilly Castle— just in better condition. I'm sure whatever you brought to wear will be perfect.' Maybe it was that gold dress from the last fundraiser. He had so many fantasies about slipping that dress from her shoulders, down her body…

Gwen didn't look convinced, so he carried on.

'But if you're really worried, why don't we spend the day in Nantes today? I've booked a hotel there for tonight anyway, so we don't have to drive back after the fundraiser. We can go check in, scope out the château and do a little shopping. Nantes has some beautiful shops. I'm sure we could find something new to wear tonight, if you'd like.' And then they could stop for lunch. Maybe even at that little chocolatier he'd visited last time he was there… Normally, he was careful with his diet these days—but as a rugby player he needed a ridiculous number of calories anyway. This weekend he figured he could let himself indulge a little.

Gwen picked up her *pain au chocolat*. 'You want to take me shopping?'

He smiled. 'I want to show you Nantes. And if I get to see you in beautiful dresses too, that's just an added bonus in my book.'

She considered for a moment, then nodded. 'Okay, then.'

* * *

Traffic in Nantes was stop-start, and he'd forgotten how tight the multi-storey car park was for his four-by-four, but once they were parked they were close to everything that mattered—lunch, shops and the château.

'We'll have a little wander around first,' he told Gwen, as they climbed out of the car. 'It's a pretty town to spend time in. I think you'll like it.'

He hoped she would, anyway. Even if things didn't work out between them, he'd meant what he'd said about her and Evie using his home. Maybe they'd even visit with his parents. There were beaches not too far a drive away, and a farm that had llamas and goats and giant rabbits he thought Evie would love...

They walked up the street towards Nantes Cathedral first. Ryan had never been much of one for architecture, or religion when it came down to it. But there was something about that place that sent a shiver down his back— as if he was close to a world other than his own. He'd wandered in there one of his first days off alone in France, exploring Nantes as a way to stop obsessing about everything he'd left behind, and had somehow found himself sitting in one of the wooden pews for almost an hour, just thinking.

Looking back, that was probably the moment his changes had started.

He owed a lot to that lump of stone and stained glass.

'It's beautiful,' Gwen said, as they approached the steps. 'Do you think we could go in?'

He nodded. 'Of course.'

Inside, he let Gwen explore the columns and the smaller chapels, the stained glass and the tombs, while he took a seat and just soaked up the atmosphere. They'd been together constantly—apart from while they'd slept—since they'd left Wales. Maybe she needed a little alone time.

As far as he knew, Gwen wasn't really very religious either, but he watched her light a candle all the same. For George, he supposed.

The cathedral was peaceful and calm, but the war inside Ryan still raged. The part that told him he wasn't good enough to even *look* at Gwen. The part that hated himself for wanting his brother's wife. For thinking he could ever be a good enough man to have her for his own.

He wasn't George. He'd never be George. George had been golden and perfect and naturally everything Ryan had needed to fight and scrape to become. And even then he knew he wasn't close to George's level.

He didn't blame his parents for cutting him out of their lives after the funeral, especially given the hurtful words they'd thrown at each other. George had been their perfect son, and Ryan hadn't been there to save him from the accident that had ended his career. He hadn't been there to help him recover. He hadn't been in the bar that night when George had played hero, stepping in to stop a fight, and been stabbed. And given which one of them had more normally been in Cardiff bars... Ryan had never really understood why George had been there at all. But he knew that his brother would always be the one to stop a fight, not join in, like *he* would have done back then. George had made them proud. *He*'d only let them down, over and over again.

He could never replace George—for Gwen or for his parents. But he hoped the person he'd grown up into might find his own place in their hearts.

Gwen slipped into the pew beside him, looking up at the altar. 'This is a special place, isn't it?'

'Yeah.' His voice sounded raspy, even to his own ears.

Suddenly, Gwen's hand was in his, squeezing tight. And Ryan knew, at that moment, that he was closer than ever to being the man he hoped to be.

A man worthy of his brother's memory.

Nantes was beautiful.

From the cathedral, where Ryan sat so peacefully while she explored, to the cobbled streets they walked down, filled with antique shops and jewellery shops, towards the Château des Ducs de Bretagne, so she could see where she'd be partying that evening.

'Wow.' She'd been impressed by Ryan's 'little *manoir*', but this place was something else, and she was more certain than ever that the gold dress she'd brought—the same one she'd worn for every fundraiser she'd attended that year—wasn't fancy enough for an event here.

From the street outside the stone walls and towers dominated, their fairy-tale turrets pointed against the bright blue, late spring sky. The château was alive with visitors, exploring the grounds, sitting in the late spring sunshine on the grass by the side of the moat. Gwen could have just leaned against the wall and people-watched for hours.

'Come on.' Ryan grabbed her hand again—something he'd been doing on and off since the cathedral, when she'd taken his. She wasn't going to deny the tiny thrill that raced through her every time his fingers wrapped around hers. 'Let's look inside.'

As they crossed the stone bridge over the moat, something silver glinted in the sunshine. Gwen stopped and stared. 'Is that... is that a slide?'

Ryan laughed. 'Yep. It runs from the walls to down by the moat. Want to try it?'

'Uh...no, thanks.' The height of the thing was terrifying. 'Let's just go in, yeah?'

Inside the château's walls, the stonework was all painted a blinding white. The courtyard housed an old well, a museum and a gift shop, and there were steps up to the walls for visitors to walk around. Gwen took in the sheer scale of the place and tried to imagine how it would look tonight for the fundraiser.

She couldn't.

They wandered around the outside of the courtyard, then out through another gate over the moat, where Gwen was delighted to find a small family of turtles sunning themselves on the rocks. Then they headed around the moat and back into the city to find her something to wear.

Realistically, Gwen knew that hardly any-body would be paying attention to what she wore tonight. The gold dress—familiar, comfortable, and something she knew she looked good in—would probably be fine. That was why she'd packed it, after all.

But now she was here in France, with Ryan, it just didn't feel…enough. She wanted to wear something that gave her the kind of confidence that had never come naturally to her. Something she felt beautiful in.

Something that would turn Ryan speechless, for preference.

'Don't worry,' Ryan had said, as they'd walked through the streets of Nantes, back past the antiques shops and craft shops and tourist shops—and no dress shops. 'I know just the place.'

Gwen had, to be honest, doubted him. In her experience of the women who appeared on Ryan's arm—mostly seen through the papers, she had to admit—they were more often dressed for a hen night in Cardiff than a swanky fundraiser in a château.

But as she stood looking up at the nineteenth-century interior of the Passage Pommeraye, she conceded she might have been wrong to prejudge him—again.

The arching glass roof, the columns, the

balconies, the sweeping staircase, the black railings against the white stone, and boutique after boutique selling everything she could possibly need—and a lot of things she wouldn't.

'Okay,' she said, turning around to get a good look at everything. 'This should work.'

It took them a mere three shops to find a dress she thought might be appropriate for the occasion. Ryan had tried to persuade her to try things on in the previous two shops, but Gwen knew what suited her, and what she liked. There was no point trying something different.

But this dress…this dress was worth a try.

She shimmied into it in the small, curtained dressing room, smoothing it over her curves as she studied herself in the mirror.

The dress was a creamy, almost buttery colour, with beading across the bodice that shimmered in the lights. The skirts were chiffon, falling in a waterfall of layers down to her ankles.

Yes, this would do very nicely indeed.

The look in Ryan's eyes when she stepped out in it only confirmed her decision. *This* was what she'd wanted to go dress shopping for. The confidence she felt when Ryan couldn't look away from her.

She'd spent the last few years building up her own confidence in herself, her competence, and the ability to keep everything—life, family, work, Evie—going by herself. But here, in France, she didn't have to do it alone any more. She could have Ryan at her side, looking at her like she was the only woman in the world.

She had to admit it was more than tempting to try and take that back home with her too.

'You're so beautiful.' He stepped forward, seemingly automatically to put his hands at her waist.

'Think I'll do?' she asked, smiling up at him.

In response, he bent his head and kissed her, slow and deep and filled with longing.

He finally broke away as a shop assistant cleared her throat, and Gwen grinned.

'Better find some matching shoes then,' she said.

CHAPTER EIGHT

THE COURTYARD OF the Château des Ducs de Bretagne sparkled in the fading sunlight. Fairy lights had been wrapped around potted trees that circled the open space, with a larger centrepiece of greenery and lights in the middle. The spaces in between were filled with French rugby royalty, and the sort of local prominent citizens who could be counted on to donate the big bucks.

Stalls had been set up serving drinks and waiters in bow-ties circulated with trays of champagne and canapés. Larger lights lined the upper walls, sparkling off the decorations that hung across the stonework.

But the brightest thing in the whole castle was Gwen Phillips, and Ryan could not keep his eyes off her.

They'd had a perfect day. From talking over breakfast to exploring Nantes to dress shopping to lunch at a little café on the square, listening to a violinist while they'd eaten and chatted some more. Every moment in her company was a joy, and Ryan didn't want it to end.

Not least because he didn't know exactly what they'd be to each other when they returned to Wales. He had a feeling this easy companionship between them might not translate back across the Channel, when there was Evie, his parents, rugby, and the national press to worry about.

For tonight, though, he just wanted to enjoy being with Gwen. Memorising every moment, in case they were the only ones he got.

To think he'd honestly believed he could protect his heart around her. Even if he was never anything more than her friend from today onwards, Ryan knew now it wouldn't make any difference.

He was hers. Whether she wanted him or not.

'This is so gorgeous!' Gwen's hazel eyes were wide as she stared around them. 'Do you know many people here?'

How could he tell? He'd barely even looked at anyone else since she'd walked out of her bedroom in the hotel suite he'd booked. Now he glanced around and realised that, yes, he knew these people. Lots of them, anyway.

'Uh, yeah. Want me to introduce you to some?'

She grinned. 'Absolutely. See if I can get the real story of what you were up to in France from your friends.'

She was teasing, he knew that. But, actually, that was exactly what he wanted her to do.

He wanted her to believe in the man he was now. Wanted her to want him, the way he needed her.

Spotting his friend Julienne across the courtyard, deep in conversation with a striking blonde he recognised as his wife, Marie, Ryan took Gwen's hand and led her across, snagging her a glass of champagne on the way.

'Ryan!' Julienne saw him coming and broke off his conversation to open his arms and welcome him. 'It's so good to see you, my friend! I hoped my invitation would tempt you back over the water. You see, I got roped into taking your place on the charity board...'

'I did! And it's good to see you too.' Ryan hugged him tight, then turned to Gwen. 'Julienne was one of my first friends on the team over here,' he explained. 'Julienne, this is Gwen. My...' What was she, exactly? He couldn't say sister-in-law without opening up a whole lot of questions. Although there was an outside chance people here might even recognise George's wife...was it better to be honest?

'Date,' Gwen finished for him, holding a hand out for Julienne to shake. He took it, then pulled her close to kiss both cheeks.

Date. Yeah, that worked. Why hadn't he thought of that?

Because he was nervous, he realised. He'd thought he was years past pre-game nerves or even self-doubt around women. But with Gwen, everything was different. He doubted himself, and his luck, every moment they were together.

Julienne introduced his wife, Marie, and the four of them took a tour of the courtyard, sampling canapés and enjoying the sight of the entertainers brought in for the occasion. While the other three stood raptly watching a magician doing incredible sleight of hand, Julienne disappeared to fetch drinks for them all. When he returned with three glasses of champagne and one orange juice, and handed the latter to Ryan, he caught Gwen frowning.

'Ah, our good Welsh chapel boy,' Julienne said, in a terrible impression of a Welsh accent. 'Hardly ever touches a drop these days. Didn't you know?'

Gwen laughed at the impression. 'No, I knew. I just... I don't know.'

Ryan did, though. She was surprised that everyone else knew. Back home in Wales he hadn't advertised it, but over here in France it was just part of who he was.

'I wouldn't say never a drop,' Ryan put in lightly. 'I had champagne at your wedding.'

'Half a glass, and only because you were making the toast,' Marie said, laughing. 'He was Julienne's best man, you know. He'd only known him a year, but apparently the bond between rugby boys is unbreakable.'

Julienne shrugged. 'My stag night was three days before a summer show match the powers that be arranged at the last minute. I needed someone I could trust to make sure we all made it back alive—and in a fit state to play!'

'And you picked Ryan?' Gwen asked, sounding faintly incredulous. Ryan knew without asking that she had to be remembering George's stag do in Bristol, when she'd had to come and bail them all out at four in the morning, before the papers got hold of it.

'Of course!' Julienne threw an arm around his shoulders, and Ryan remembered exactly why he and the Frenchman had become such good friends, so quickly. Julienne let him be whoever he wanted to be, and believed him when he showed that to be the real him. He'd never met anyone in Britain who did that—probably because they all knew too much of his past.

But he hoped that Gwen might be starting to, at last.

'Who else but the Great Abstainer for keeping us all in line?' Julienne joked, making them all laugh. 'Now, come on. I want to see the tumblers over there. Also, I heard that they're opening the slide later…'

'No way that could end badly,' Ryan muttered, but he was smiling as he followed them all the same.

It was gone midnight before they made it back to the hotel suite Ryan had booked for them for the night. Gwen slipped her high heels from her aching feet, glad that they didn't have the drive back to his house ahead of them—although, given that Ryan had stayed on orange juice all night, he could have driven them.

All the same, a night in a fancy hotel followed by room-service breakfast was the sort of treat she hadn't experienced since Evie was born. And it gave her the chance to consider all she'd learned about Ryan over the course of the evening at the Château des Ducs de Bretagne.

She'd half wondered, at first, if Julienne's view of Ryan was skewed because he was even more of a rogue than Ryan had been in his heyday. But spending time with him and his wife had made it clear that wasn't the case.

Gwen had known, logically, that Ryan had changed while he'd been in France. But seeing the person he was through another's eyes made that change all the more real.

And it wasn't just Julienne and Marie. Every person she'd met that night talked about a Ryan she hadn't truly dared believe existed. A responsible, respectable Ryan. The one who others turned to in order to keep his teammates in line. One who cared about his reputation, about his friends, more than he cared about his own entertainment or even well-being.

'The number of times he threw himself across the field to defend somebody. Or pulled a teammate out of a fight in a pub and got them to sober up and go home...' Julienne shook his head. 'There'd definitely have been more injuries and more police records among our team if he hadn't joined us.'

She'd wished, at that moment, that Ryan

had never left. No, not that, because then he'd never have changed at all. Never grown up.

But she'd wished that he'd been there to save George that night, not for the first time. That he'd known how his brother had struggled after his accident, and come home to help him, maybe. That he'd been in that pub and stopped George from starting whatever stupid fight he'd begun, before his opponent had ever pulled the knife that had killed him.

But he hadn't been. And there was no point raking over that past any more. No reason to tarnish Ryan's memory of his brother now it could do no good.

Gwen was done with living in the past. She'd spent the last three years stuck as Gwen Phillips, wife of golden boy George Phillips, then his widow. Pretending to the world that her marriage hadn't been broken, even before her husband had been. Masquerading as a perfect wife, taking care of her injured husband, when most days she'd just been trying to dodge his furious rages, or keep Evie out of the firing line. Ignoring the other women who'd burst into their marriage. Before the accident, she'd suspected he'd been unfaithful. Afterwards, his shifting personality hadn't even bothered to try and hide it.

Three years pretending, playing the part of a woman she wasn't any longer.

She was ready to move into the future at last.

Ryan had changed his whole self. Maybe she could too.

And she knew exactly how to start.

Ryan had left her to change in her own bedroom of the suite when they'd returned, knowing she was exhausted. But she could hear him puttering around in the lounge area, and suddenly a burst of fresh energy surged through her.

Barefoot, she padded back out of her bedroom door, leaning against the frame to watch Ryan fixing a cup of something at the suite's kitchenette. He'd taken off his jacket and tie, and his white shirt was untucked and open over his dark trousers, showing off muscles she'd only dreamed about before that night in the swimming pool.

Now she remembered how they'd felt under her fingertips, hard and defined as she'd run her hands over his bare, wet skin.

She wanted to touch him again. Tonight.

She wanted everything he'd stopped them having the night before.

Ryan turned, a cup and saucer in his hand, and visibly started to find him watching her.

'I… I made you a peppermint tea,' he said. 'Thought it might help you sleep after a busy night. You said your ears were still ringing from the noise…'

He trailed off as she pushed away from the doorframe and crossed the room towards him.

'That's sweet,' she said, taking the cup and placing it on the counter. 'But I can think of other ways you could help me to sleep well tonight.'

She held her hand against his chest, palm to muscle, and felt him tense.

'Gwen…' There was caution in his eyes. Or was it concern? For her? Or for him?

Either way, she intended to dispel it. They'd both been waiting for this long enough.

Raising herself up on tiptoe, she tilted her head up to place a kiss against his mouth, then along his jawline and running down his throat. 'Ryan,' she murmured. 'You wanted to say something?'

She felt his Adam's apple bob under her mouth as she kissed across it, then down towards his chest.

'I… We…'

'*We* want this,' she finished for him. 'Don't we?'

She only had to look up into his eyes to see

the truth of it. The depths of want there made her shiver, but only in the good way.

'Yes,' he breathed. 'God, yes. But Gwen—'

That was all she needed to know. Hands on his shoulders, she pulled herself up to kiss him again, deep and hard and desperate.

'You wanted me to be sure, to know that this wasn't just one night, right? I know that now, Ryan. So will you please just take me to bed?'

She didn't need to ask twice. Sweeping her up into his arms so fast that the whole room spun, Ryan headed straight for her bedroom again, Gwen grinning against his bare chest.

Finally, she'd have reality to test those dreams of hers against.

She had a feeling that reality would win by a mile.

The hotel bed wasn't as spectacular as the four-poster back at Le Manoir, but Gwen didn't care. The view, as Ryan placed her on the bed and knelt over her, his shirt falling open at her sides, was far superior.

His mouth was on hers again the moment she lay down, hungry and wanting, as if he'd been dreaming of this as much as she had. Perhaps he had. Gwen lost herself in his kiss, pushing his shirt from his shoulders as she rose up to meet him.

Ryan's fingers were at work divesting her of her clothes too, pulling the beautiful dress she'd chosen down her body and letting it pool on the floor before returning to slip her bra straps from her shoulders too. He kissed his way down her collarbone, to the swell of her breast, his tongue swirling around one nipple as the lace of her bra lost the battle to keep her covered. Gwen arched her back, pressing her body closer to his, wanting, needing, every inch of them to be touching.

The weeks she'd been dreaming of this felt like months, years even. Like wanting Ryan had taken over every inch of her brain, and her body.

And now she was here, she didn't want to waste a moment of it.

Her bra was gone completely now, and one of Ryan's large hands covered her right breast, while his mouth was back at her left. Sweeping her palms up the skin of his back, she fisted one hand in his dark hair as the sensations he was eliciting raced through her.

'Is this okay?' he asked, the words mumbled against her skin.

'Just don't stop,' Gwen gasped back.

For a second Ryan raised his head and shot her a wicked smile. 'As you wish,' he said.

Then he kissed a burning trail down the

hollow between her breasts, over her stomach, all the way down to between her thighs—and Gwen stopped thinking altogether.

Waking up with Gwen in his arms was, quite possibly, the best new experience Ryan had ever had the good fortune to undertake.

He didn't know how last night had matched up to the dreams she'd confessed to having about them, but it had blown his imaginings clear out of the water. The way she'd felt against him, the way they'd moved together…he'd never felt as in tune with another person, ever.

Like every barrier, every secret, every worry between them had just disappeared.

Unfortunately, there was still the real world to deal with when she woke up.

He knew the moment she came awake, because she tensed in his arms for a second before looking up at his face and relaxing.

'Sorry,' she said, pressing a kiss to his shoulder. 'It's been an awfully long time since I've woken up like this.'

Ryan held her tighter. 'That's okay. But I have to warn you, I could definitely get used to it.'

She smiled at that, but it quickly faded. 'So could I. But we've only got one more night at Le Manoir. Then it will be back to the real world.'

'We'll still be the same people in the real world that we are right now,' Ryan pointed out.

'I suppose so.'

The hesitation in her voice pricked his heart. He'd been so sure last night that this was what she wanted—that *he* was what she wanted. Not just for one night at a fancy fundraiser, or a weekend away in France. But for good, the way he wanted her.

The way he realised now that he'd *always* wanted her.

He knew relationships took more than a couple of nights away from reality. He knew that the real world posed more challenges than they'd found here in France. He just didn't think that was a reason not to try.

Of course, he'd never really managed a proper, grown-up relationship before. He'd been more of a fast fling kind of guy. But that was before Gwen.

Hunkering down under the covers, Ryan turned on his side, until his nose was almost touching hers and he could see straight into her eyes. 'Tell me what's going on in there,' he said, smoothing a hand over her caramel hair.

'Nothing,' she said, but he knew she was lying.

'Is it Evie? My parents?'

Sighing, Gwen twisted to bury her head in the pillow. 'Both?'

Ryan flopped onto his back again, and ran a hand up and down her spine. 'That's fair. I know there's a lot of things we'll need to figure out. But I have faith that we can do it.'

There was no other option for him. He wanted the life he'd been dreaming of for too long now. He'd earned it. Not Gwen. She wasn't something to be earned, exactly. She was something he hoped he'd prove worthy of every day, ideally for the rest of his life. Not that he tell her that just yet. Still too soon.

But he wanted his home back. He wanted his family back. And even he had to admit that being with Gwen would make all those things easier.

She hadn't answered him, though. 'Do you?'

'Do I what?' Gwen asked, peeking up from the pillow.

'Have faith. In us.' He was holding his breath, Ryan realised. This answer mattered, for him, and for their future.

But Gwen gave him a wicked smile, and suddenly he felt her hands running low over his body. 'I have complete faith that you can make me scream again before it's time to check out.'

And as much as he wanted to continue the conversation, as much as he feared there was something she wasn't telling him—something that mattered a lot—his body overruled his mind as she grabbed the part of him that always tended to do the thinking in situations like this.

They had the whole drive back to Le Manoir, not to mention the journey back to Wales, to talk. He was probably overthinking things, anyway. Rushing her. She just needed time to adjust to things between them, that was probably it. After all, he'd been thinking about this a lot longer than she had.

George had been the love of her life, and it took time to move on from that. But Ryan knew, deep down, that his brother would want Gwen to be happy. That he wouldn't want her to be alone for the rest of her life.

He hoped George might even want the same for him.

But those were conversations for other, less interesting times. Right now, they just needed to enjoy this time together.

They'd figure out all the rest of it later.

CHAPTER NINE

THEIR LAST TWENTY-FOUR hours in France were positively blissful.

They missed breakfast at the hotel, but given what they were doing instead Gwen decided she could live with that. Besides, they stopped at a lovely little café for a late brunch before the drive back to Ryan's *manoir*.

There, they made the most of their last hours together in style. And in the swimming pool. And on the sheepskin rug in front of the fire. And most definitely in her four-poster bed. And his.

Gwen had got dressed only for the purpose of video-calling Evie. Otherwise clothing had definitely been surplus to requirements.

Best of all, she'd managed to distract Ryan from any more deep and meaningful conversations about their future together. Oh, she knew they were coming, but she didn't want to waste time on them now. Not when she knew how much harder it would be to get this kind of time alone once they were home in Wales again.

A couple of days away with Uncle Ryan, to attend an important fundraiser to help with the trust, was something Evie could just about understand—and Gwen's parents-in-law too, for that matter. Uncle Ryan staying over in Mummy and Daddy's bed was a whole different matter. And if she as much as saw them kiss Gwen knew she'd report it to her grandparents in no time. And why shouldn't she? It was her life and she got to share the things that happened in it. Gwen would never ask her daughter to lie or keep secrets for her.

But now she was on the Eurostar back home again, she couldn't help but let the worries fill her. If she was honest, she'd been concerned about it ever since Joe had sent her that photo of her and Ryan at the bachelor auction in Cardiff, although she'd managed to push it aside for a day or so.

The problems were obvious. Yes, her time here in France had shown her that Ryan had changed, and that his friends and colleagues here respected and trusted him to be the man they'd needed him to be. And she genuinely believed that she could too.

Back home in Wales, though, no one else would believe that.

Everyone there—Ryan's parents included—would still see the man they used to know. The one from all those awful tabloid photos, and the disciplinary hearings that had followed. And so they'd be talked about, followed, photographed. Eventually, Gwen was sure they'd come to see the truth that she had—that Ryan wasn't the same man who'd left the country three years ago. But seeing that would take time.

And in the meantime she didn't want Evie exposed to that sort of publicity and propaganda. She didn't want her to hear that talk. Couldn't risk the gossip and the scandal of her being involved with her former brother-in-law—because didn't that just play into what people already believed about him? That he'd steal his brother's wife? Never mind that she went willingly...

She knew that Ryan would understand all that if she explained. Maybe he'd even be willing to take things slowly enough to mitigate some of the fallout. She hoped so.

But that didn't solve her biggest mental block.

George.

Not just the idea of moving on from her

husband, let alone with his brother. That much she'd managed—probably helped along by the fact that in the last couple of years of their marriage there hadn't been much of a marriage between them at all.

But Ryan didn't know that. To him, George was still perfect. His idol and hero. The man he wanted to live up to. And if they were really going to do this, be a couple, eventually she was going to have to tell him the truth.

She *really* didn't want to tell him the truth. Didn't want him to know the man his hero had become, even if the bulk of the blame for it lay with a brain injury he couldn't have helped. She didn't want to be the one to shatter his illusions.

She'd hidden the reality of George's personality change from everyone she could, especially those who would be hurt by it, like Evie and his parents. She'd told herself she was doing it for their own good, to protect them. But now she worried that wasn't her only reason.

She'd been protecting her pride too.

However much Anita Chowdhury taught her about the impact and consequences of brain injuries, their effect on a sufferer's personality, and however much Gwen understood, intellectually, that it wasn't her fault, or George's, it didn't stop the way it made her feel.

She hadn't been enough to bring George back from the place his accident had taken him. That was what it came down to. And while she knew logically that most of those changes—the rages, the affairs, the cruel words—had been brought around by his accident, deep in her heart she knew that wasn't the whole of it.

Because the part she'd never told anyone, not even Joe, was that the end of her marriage had started before the tackle that had ended his career. If he hadn't been injured, she didn't know now if they'd even still be married.

She shook the thought away, not wanting to remember those arguments, the way he'd given everything to rugby, his training, his team, and kept nothing back for them. How she'd honestly believed all those nights out with the boys had been genuinely about team building and nothing more—until she'd found the first of the text messages from a woman he'd spent the night with.

George had been the golden boy of rugby. And maybe he'd hidden his flaws better than his brother ever had. But he hadn't been perfect.

Even if her pride wouldn't allow her to let other people see that. She didn't want pity now he was dead, and she hadn't wanted it then either.

She couldn't bear to see the pain and disappointment—and probably disbelief—in Meredith and Dylan's eyes. Couldn't think of Evie growing up thinking her father had been anything but a hero.

Knowing that he'd started the fight that had killed him, over a woman who hadn't been his wife.

And she wouldn't see Ryan cursing his brother for hurting her, or wondering why she'd stayed.

Or worse…she hated herself for even thinking it, but she knew there was another fear inside her too.

She knew people could change—and she believed Ryan had. But George had changed, as well. And she couldn't help the small part of her that worried that, if Ryan had changed once, he could change back again.

'You're thinking hard over there,' Ryan said, from the train seat opposite her. 'Anything you want to share?'

She flashed him a smile she hoped looked authentic, and shook her head. 'Just wool-gathering,' she said, returning to staring out of the window.

The problem was, soon, she was going to have to do something with all that wool.

They'd caught the very early train back to England, and hit Kings Cross St Pancras station just as everyone else was starting their working day. The minute they stepped out onto the platform, though, Gwen's phone started pinging. She reached for it—but then spotted a newspaper stand carrying the daily free paper for London, and realised she didn't need to read the messages.

She already knew what they'd be about.

There, on the front cover, was a photo of her late husband. Beside him a photo of a woman she didn't recognise holding a small child.

And the headline: *'Golden Boy of Rugby Fathered My Baby!'*

Apparently the time for wool-gathering was over.

She needed to make some decisions. And fast.

Ryan took a couple of steps before he realised that Gwen wasn't beside him. Frowning, he turned to find her standing stock still behind him on the platform, staring at something.

'Gwen? Are you okay?' He was by her side in an instant, and only once she nodded did he turn to find out what she was staring at.

Golden Boy of Rugby Fathered My Baby!

Ryan barked a laugh at the ridiculousness of it. Anyone who'd known George knew he'd been besotted with his wife, and obsessed with doing the right thing. The very idea that he'd strayed was absurd.

Only Gwen wasn't laughing.

'Gwen? Don't even waste time looking at it. You knew George better than anyone. He wouldn't do something like that. It's just someone fishing for a pay-out from the tabloids, that's all.'

'It…it might not be,' she said, her voice slow and shocked. Then she turned to him, jerky but fast. 'We need to get home, Ryan. We need to get to your parents before they see this.'

He stared at her too-pale face. She genuinely believed this. And that…that put doubt in his heart too.

There had to be a simple explanation. He just couldn't imagine right now what it could be.

'Okay. We'll grab a cab to Paddington.'

Practical planning, that was what they needed now. 'But, Gwen… I'm going to need you to explain this.' If there even *was* a reasonable explanation for the impossible.

How could it possibly be true? Ryan had *known* his brother. Had spent his whole life trying to be half the man he was. This *couldn't* be true.

Dragging their cases behind them, they headed for the outside world and the taxi rank. Almost as an afterthought, Ryan grabbed a copy of the paper on his way.

He needed to understand this.

'Okay,' he said, as soon as they were settled in the cab, with their luggage in the boot, and on their way to Paddington station. 'Tell me what's going on that could possibly make you believe this is true.'

He held up the newspaper and she tugged it away, placing it face down on the seat next to her and casting a nervous glance at the driver.

The driver, who was swearing at someone who'd just pulled out in front of them, couldn't have cared less, Ryan was pretty certain. But the fact that Gwen was worried that he would concerned him.

'Gwen. Talk to me.' Glad he'd taken one of the fold-down, rear-facing seats in the black cab, he reached across to hold her hands. She had to look at him here, couldn't hide.

And he had a feeling he needed to see her face as she told him this story.

'George…after the accident, he wasn't the same. He couldn't play rugby, which he hated, and the rehabilitation on his arm was slow, even getting him back to normal function was a struggle.'

'I remember.' He'd hated seeing his brother that way, stuck in a hospital bed at first, then fighting to gain full mobility back in his badly broken arm. He'd mostly got reports on his rehabilitation from Gwen, or his mother, back when they were both still speaking to him. George had been too proud to show that kind of weakness to the brother he still resented for leaving.

Gwen worried her lower lip with her teeth. 'But it wasn't just the break. The head injury…that was more of a problem.'

'It was?' Ryan frowned. As far as he recalled, there'd been no mention of that, once the initial fear and concussion had passed. He knew there was *always* concern about repeated head injuries in rugby—and rightly so, given when he'd learned from Anita Chowdhury. The terrifying hours when George hadn't regained consciousness had seemed to last for ever. But once George had come round and they'd set his arm he'd assumed the danger had passed.

'He… His personality changed. Well, perhaps intensified is a better word. We'd… Oh, God.' Closing her eyes, she tipped her head back against the seat. 'I've never told anyone this. But…we'd been having some problems even before his accident.'

'What sort of problems?' Every muscle in his body felt too tense to move. Gwen and George had been the perfect couple. If *they'd* had problems, what hope was there for *him* and Gwen?

'He… Rugby was everything to him— especially after he was made captain. I was home with Evie and feeling neglected, I guess. I nagged him, asked him to put us first for a change—but he only started staying out longer, and more often. Then I started finding text messages from other women on his phone—'

'God, Gwen, no. There must have been an explanation! George loved you! He wouldn't….'

Oh, God, but what if he had?

'His explanation was that I was a nightmare to be married to, apparently.' She gave a small shrug, her whole expression so beaten down that Ryan couldn't help but shift to the seat next to her and wrap his arms around her. 'I was about to confront him after the match, the day he had his accident. But after that... how could I? All I cared about was getting him well again. I figured if we stuck together through it, I'd get my husband back.'

'What happened next?' Ryan asked, knowing, instinctively, that this story wasn't over. It didn't end until his brother's funeral. Or until an unknown woman appeared in the papers claiming she'd had George Phillips's son.

Outside, London traffic was sluggish, and the cab stop-started its way to Paddington. There was no way they could get back to Cardiff before his parents saw the papers, or before one of them called them. He thought Gwen must realise that. But, still, she looked anxiously out of the window at the slow-moving traffic.

'He was so angry—about the tackle, about his arm. And then when he realised his career in international rugby was over, and that he might never even make it back to playing for his team... I mean, of course he was furious and frustrated. And it took a while for me to even realise that some of the...changes in his personality were to do with his head injury, rather than just what had happened to him.'

Ryan shook his head. 'When I spoke to friends who'd visited…they said he just seemed like himself. Annoyed to be stuck recovering, but he was always like that after an injury. Couldn't wait to get back out on the pitch.'

'That's what I wanted people to believe. I… I wanted people to remember George as he was. As I hoped he would be again.'

'But then he went and threw himself into stopping that fight—' Something in her expression cut him off.

George had been stabbed trying to stop a fight. That was what he'd been told. What everyone had been told. What he'd believed.

But, then, he'd believed that Gwen and George had had the perfect marriage too.

'Gwen. What happened the night George died?'

She wouldn't look at him. 'He…he stormed out to go to the pub that night. I don't even know who with—I don't think it was any of the boys from the team. But he'd started making all sorts of new friends by then. He never introduced me to any of them.' She swallowed, so hard he could watch her throat move. 'The police said…witnesses told them he started a fight with some guy over a comment he made about a woman, I think. Just…

launched himself at him. People started piling in, someone called the police, and...'

'Someone else pulled a knife.'

That could have been him. That was the only thought in Ryan's head for a moment. That if he'd carried on the way he'd started in Cardiff, if he hadn't moved to France, that could so easily have been him.

His second thought was, *I should have been there to stop him.*

No wonder his mother hated him so. Wait... 'Do Mum and Dad know the truth?'

'Which part?'

'Any of it?' Because Ryan had a suspicion he wasn't the only one she'd been keeping the truth about his brother from.

Her wince confirmed it. 'They loved him so much. I couldn't take that away from them. They'd already lost him, Ryan, I didn't see what good it would do.'

But as the taxi pulled up outside Paddington station, the truth of what it might have done hit him, hard, in the chest.

It might have made his parents able to love *him* again.

Gwen's heart hurt, reliving those terrible few years. And telling it all to Ryan...well, that hurt a hell of a lot more.

She'd been holding in all these truths for so long it was hard to let them out. Even Joe, who knew how George had been after his accident, didn't understand that it had started earlier. In so many ways it had been easier to blame the head injury for making George the man he'd become. And she knew that a lot of it—the angry flashes he hadn't been able to control, the lashing out, the irrational rages—had been due to that.

But the cheating on her... That had come earlier. That couldn't be blamed on anything other than George being human and flawed.

Something she'd worked so hard to never admit, before now.

She saw it—the moment Ryan realised what she'd done. And she recognised it too, because in that same moment *she* realised the depth of it.

The echoes of George's behaviour and her own choices, ricocheting into the future to ruin this new happiness they'd found together.

She hadn't just knocked George off his pedestal when she'd shown Ryan the reality of his brother as a man, not a god. She'd taken away part of Ryan's belief system, and the reasoning behind so much of his life. The choices he'd made, the person he'd become, so much of that had been tied up in who his brother was.

And now he knew that George had never been that person at all.

What would that do to a man?

But it went deeper than that, she knew. Ryan hadn't just spent his whole life either trying to live up to or be the opposite of his brother. He'd spent it in his shadow, unable to climb out of the darkness it had cast.

He'd been compared to George from the day he was born, and not generally favourably.

If his parents had known the truth about George, might they have looked more kindly on their younger son? Could they have reconciled much sooner than now? It was too late to know. But she was damn sure that Ryan was thinking it.

Ryan paid the taxi driver without looking at her, and Gwen climbed out of the car and waited to retrieve her suitcase. She left the newspaper lying on the seat behind her. She didn't need the reminder. Her heart was reminder enough. The tattered remnants of it anyway. The ones that had just started to mend, under Ryan's gentle care.

But she couldn't think about that now. This was bigger than a fledgling romance that made her feel wanted for the first time in ages. It was bigger than her heart and what *she* wanted.

This was about her family.

She had to get back to Cardiff before Evie heard something she shouldn't about her dad. Before she had to deal with reporters at the door or calling incessantly, the way they had after his death.

The man was dead and buried. Why couldn't people let him rest?

Why couldn't they let *her* rest? Or at least move on with her life. Maybe even find some happiness somewhere.

But not with Ryan, she could see that now. Saw it in the lines of his back as he stalked towards their platform. In the set of his shoulders as they took their seats. In the way he couldn't quite meet her eyes as the train around them filled with other passengers.

Oh, this journey was going to be absolute hell.

Just this morning, he'd been kissing every inch of her body, worshipping her with his mouth, his hands.

Now he couldn't even look at her. And she couldn't blame him either.

She wanted to believe he was just processing everything she'd told him. But she tried to make a point of not lying to herself, even if she wasn't always entirely honest with the other people in her life.

It was over for them. Before it had really even started.

Because her actions had ruined any chance he had of reconciling with his parents before now. Because she'd lied to him, and to everyone else.

But mostly because she still couldn't bring herself to let Evie have her image of her perfect dad ruined by the truth.

CHAPTER TEN

THE ENGLISH COUNTRYSIDE sped past the train windows, rain splattered and endlessly green. Ryan longed for the rugged purple mountains and rugged coastline of Wales, but even racing towards it didn't feel entirely like going home.

Home was where George was, except George was gone, and somehow hadn't ever been the man he imagined. Home was where his parents were, except they still loved a fiction and refused to see the real man Ryan had become.

Home, he'd have said last night, was in Gwen's arms. Now he could hardly look at her. Not until he'd sorted through this whole mess in his head.

It wasn't her fault, he knew that. She'd been trying to save her marriage, to look after her family. To protect Evie. He couldn't blame her for any of that.

Except, deep down, he knew he did.

How different might the last few years have been for him if he'd known the truth? If he'd suspected for a moment that George wasn't the perfect golden boy everyone believed him to be? If his *parents* had known that?

He might never have left Wales. He might have helped his brother—even saved him. He might not have fallen out so hideously with his parents at George's funeral, at least.

Everything could have been different.

He could have been different.

Would he have still acted up so dreadfully, desperate for his parents' attention, if George hadn't been so impossibly perfect? Would he have grown to be something other than the black sheep of the family if George hadn't been so white?

Finally, he turned to find Gwen watching him, owlishly, looking like a bird about to take flight if he made a loud noise. She was scared, he realised. Not of him, he hoped, but of the truths she'd shared.

'Okay, what I need to know is this,' he started—but her eyes widened in alarm and she tipped her head towards the woman sitting across the aisle from them. The one reading another newspaper with George's face plastered on the front. As Ryan looked over, the woman glanced up, her eyes narrowing as she saw him, as if trying to place his face.

He turned away, angling his face towards the window.

'So we're not going to talk about this,' he murmured softly.

'Not here,' she whispered back, urgency in her voice. 'Please, Ryan. Not here.'

He nodded sharply. 'In that case, I'm going to go find the buffet car. I need a drink.'

He didn't ask if she wanted anything, didn't wait to see if she would come with him. He just stalked in what he hoped was the right direction, taking all his fury with him.

He needed time to process this. And by his reckoning, he had until they reached Cardiff to do so. Because then they needed to face his parents—and he needed to know what she was going to do next.

They'd have seen the news, the accusations—there was no way they could avoid it. Too many of Mum's 'friends' would have called to check she had, under the guise of wanting to make sure she was okay. And that was before you got to the local journalists calling to try their luck.

Would Gwen tell them the same truths she'd told him? Or would she keep lying?

Keep the fiction of his perfect brother alive, even now he was gone?

He didn't know.

He reached the buffet car at last, and stared at the miniature bottles of spirits and single glasses of wine behind the counter. Then he ordered a coffee, because he needed to drive when they reached Cardiff, and if ever he needed his wits about him it was today.

Ryan put the suitcases in the boot of his car in silence, then climbed into the driver's seat. It was hard to imagine that just a few days ago they'd been setting off with such hope. Now, as he pulled away and began the familiar drive to his parents' house, it was all about damage limitation.

'I need to know what you're going to tell my parents.'

'What they already believe,' Gwen replied, staring out of the opposite window. 'That it's a load of rubbish intended to stir up trouble and we mustn't let Evie get wind of it and become distressed.'

'Have you heard from them this morning?'

'Your mum sent a text first thing. Said not to read the papers today as she didn't want me upset.' Gwen sounded guilty just saying it.

'Trying to protect you the same way you're protecting them, huh?'

'I guess so.'

They spent the rest of the drive the way they'd spent their train journey—in silence. He hated it. But right now he honestly had no idea what to say.

All these years, he'd imagined what might have happened if he hadn't left Gwen at the bar to go take that shot. If George hadn't swooped in and charmed her.

But now he was revisiting all the major events of his life from another, different 'what if.'

What if he'd known George wasn't so perfect? What if his parents had?

It was as different a life as the one in which he got Gwen's number that night, instead of George.

When they pulled up outside his parents' house, they sat in silence for a moment, just staring out the windscreen at the falling rain. Earlier, he'd imagined that this would be the moment they returned to reality after their perfect days away. The moment he hoped they'd decide to force reality to suit *them*, to allow them to be together.

Now he realised that reality had barged in

and ruined things, far sooner than either of them had been ready for.

'We'd better go in,' he said, unfastening his seat belt.

But Gwen paused. 'Are you sure you want to? I mean, it might not be the best time…'

'Right. Of course.' Heaven forbid he visit his *own parents*. Because they still believed he was the black sheep, the bad son, the one who had let his brother die alone because he'd left the country to try and find himself, away from the golden boy's shadow.

Because that was what Gwen *wanted* them to believe.

If Gwen got her way he would *always* be the black sheep. The disappointment. The son who let them all down. No matter how much good he did now, however hard he worked to overcome his past transgressions, none of it would matter.

They'd been assigned their roles, and Gwen would make sure they stuck to them. George, the hero. Her, the tragic widow. And him…

No. He couldn't be that person any more. Not even for her.

He turned to face her, hoping the rain hid them from view if there were any nosy paparazzi floating around out there, braving the weather. The two of them wouldn't make the front pages of the papers, not like the allegations about George, but they'd be on the local gossip websites for sure.

'Gwen, how long do you think you can keep this up?'

'As long as I have to.' She was so *stubborn*. Why hadn't he remembered that when he'd been idealising her over in France?

'You can't! Mum and Dad have to know the truth, deep down. Enough of these stories surface…now this one's out there, you can't tell me there won't be more. People love a bandwagon like this to jump on. Soon it won't matter if they're real or not! And someone is bound to come out with the real story about how George died sooner or later. Isn't it better to just tell them the truth now? Get it over with?'

'No!' Gwen cried, twisting round towards him. 'Because if I admit it, even once, that makes it real. And if it's real then Evie will have to know eventually. And she *idolises* her father. Your mum has shown her news clippings and videos and photos of him every day since he died, talking about what a great man he was. If she loses that… She's already lost the man himself. Can't she keep the memory?'

'But it's not real! And you know no person is perfect, Gwen. Not even George.' He'd thought *she* was, but he should have known better.

'Don't you think I know that?' she yelled. Her hands were clenched into fists on her thighs, and he reached out to cover them with his own. He figured he had one last chance to get through to her.

One more attempt to make her see sense. To accept the past and move on to the future— with him.

He just hoped to heaven that it worked.

Frustration oozed out of Ryan, from the tension in his shoulders to the fists clenched against his thighs.

'Gwen, think about it. If this woman really did have George's child, there are ways she can prove it. She could try to claim money from his insurance pay-out. She might want Evie to know her half-sibling—then what will you do?'

Why wouldn't he just stop? Why not just walk away and give up on all of this? Why did he keep trying to *reason* with her, of all things?

Because he's in love with you.

He'd never said the words, but Gwen knew it all the same. She'd finally recognised that look behind his eyes, the one that had been there since the day he'd returned from France. The one that had practically glowed out of him the morning they'd woken up together in Nantes.

He loved her.

Even worse, she knew she was falling in love with him too.

And she was going to tear it all apart to protect Evie, and her own damn pride.

'Then I would deal with it,' she said flatly. 'Somehow.'

'Gwen—'

'No, Ryan. Listen. I know what I'm doing here, okay?'

Don't believe me, her mind screamed. *I have no idea!*

But she'd set this plan so long ago, and she didn't know what to do but to follow it now. To keep living the life a past version of herself had decided on. Even if things had changed.

She took a breath, and kept talking. 'If I can make the George Phillips Trust a success, then it won't matter what people say about him any more. His name will be out there, representing good things, making the world a better place. A safer place, even.'

'And even if things do come out you can blame it all on his head injury, and claim that's why you're working so hard to help others in the same situation.' Ryan shook his head, a look of disbelief on his face. 'God, I should have seen this so much sooner. You're trying to rewrite the past.'

'And aren't you? Going abroad and starting again as a whole new person—and now you're trying to come back here pretending that nothing you did before even happened!' It was a low blow, and she knew it. But she was on the defensive now, and she couldn't stop herself.

'That's not what I'm doing! I came back to prove— Oh, what does it even matter now?' He raked a hand through his hair. 'Gwen, I came back because I've finally put my past behind me. I'm ready to move on with the rest of my life. With being the man I always hoped I could be but somehow could never find. I think I've found him now. And if you'll let me, I'll spend the rest of my life being that man for you because—'

'Don't say it,' she interrupted, trying to stop him. But it was no good.

'Because I love you, Gwen Phillips.'

She'd already known it, but it hit her like a punch to the gut all the same. Like a heavy tackle, bringing her to the ground until she saw stars.

And the worst part was that it couldn't matter any more.

'I love you, and I want to be with you,' Ryan went on, each word strong and deliberate. 'But I can't live in the past with you. I can't live, pretending. I've worked too hard to find who I am and what I want to be to start now. If you want another George—'

'No! I don't. Ryan, please…' The last thing she wanted was to rehash her last relationship. When it had been good, it had been everything. But when things had changed…

Ryan had already changed. He'd become the person he was meant to be, she could see that now.

She just wasn't sure that *she* had yet.

'If you want another George, I can't be him. I can't be anyone other than who I am.' He met her gaze head on, and she knew he meant every word. 'If that's enough for you, you know where to find me.' He opened the door and stepped out into the rain to open the boot and retrieve her suitcase.

And just like that, it was over. Because how could she tell him he *was* enough when she couldn't be open about their relationship, not if she wanted to protect George's legacy?

Climbing out of the car, she pulled her hood up over her hair and half her face, and took her suitcase from him. There was no kiss goodbye, not even a hug. Instead, he just gave her a sad smile as she turned and headed into the house.

And everything about it felt wrong.

Her mother-in-law was waiting with the door open before Gwen could knock, before Ryan had even got back in his car and driven away through the pouring rain.

'What were you doing, sitting out there with Ryan so long?' Meredith stripped the wet coat from her shoulders and hung it to dry, fussing around Gwen and shepherding her towards the lounge. 'I know he's helping you with the trust but, really, Gwen. You want to be careful, you know. People will talk. Especially with all this nonsense in the papers about George. They love to look for a scandal, don't they? And, heaven knows, Ryan's brought enough of them to our door already. I know you think he can be a good man like his brother, and you're a good person for thinking so, but, Gwen, I think you need to reconsider including him in the fundraising for George's trust. He's my own son, and I'll always love him, but you can't ignore the fact he only ever seems to bring trouble.'

Except this time the trouble was all George and Gwen. And she couldn't even tell Meredith that. Would she ever be able to see the new man Ryan had become?

'Where's Evie?' Gwen asked, casting around for her daughter. Normally she'd have been climbing all over her by now, and more than anything Gwen wanted to hug her, hold her close, and remind herself what she was doing all this for. *Who* she was doing it for.

'Oh, she fell asleep on the sofa with Taid, watching some movie about pirates or something. Now, about Ryan.' There was an awkward pause as Meredith gave her a meaningful look. 'I really do think that you spending time with him will only bring up more horrible rumours about George. We both know that he wasn't…quite himself after his accident. It's not fair to his memory to let these people say these things, though. Have you spoken to his lawyer yet?'

Wasn't quite himself.

Understatement of the century and yet…it was still the very first time Gwen had heard Meredith admit that George had ever been less than perfect. And Meredith had told her not to read the papers—but obviously knew she would have. Perhaps even knew that Gwen wouldn't be surprised by the stories.

Gwen stared at her, blinking away a fog that seemed to have descended too many years ago. But suddenly she saw things more clearly. Saw the panic behind Meredith's eyes, the tremor in her fingers.

And she knew.

'You…you're worried these stories are true, aren't you?' she said. 'Why? What do you know?'

'Of course they're not true!' Meredith said indignantly. But she changed course and steered Gwen into the kitchen where they couldn't be overheard. 'Not this little hussy claiming George gave her a baby, and none of the others either.'

'What…what others?'

Meredith waved a hand. 'Oh, barely a week goes by without someone telling me some dreadful story about my sons. It always used to be Ryan, but since he left they moved on to George. The difference is that when they were about Ryan I believed them. Now, when they're about George, I know better.'

'Do you?' Gwen watched her mother-in-law carefully. She knew Meredith's tells, knew when she was lying about how much sugar she'd given Evie in an afternoon, or why things had to be done the way she wanted.

'Well, George would never do such a thing, would he?' Her gaze darted around the room as she answered, flying past a photo of

George and her on the wall, and Gwen knew instantly she was lying.

'Meredith.'

'And even if they were true, what does it matter now? He's dead, isn't he? Can't they let us have his memory?' Her voice grew higher with every word, a desperation in it Gwen hadn't heard since the funeral. 'He was my perfect boy!'

'Nobody is perfect, Meredith,' Gwen said slowly. 'Not even George.'

He'd hated being held to that standard, Gwen remembered now. Resented that he could never put a foot wrong without uproar, while Ryan got away with it every week. If the brothers had ever talked about it, maybe they'd have realised that *neither* of them had had it all that easy. It was no excuse for either of their behaviours, but perhaps they'd have been better brothers for realising it.

George had wanted a freedom that the golden boy, the perfect son, had never been allowed—but he'd taken it anyway. Ryan had wanted the recognition, to be a person in his own right, not just in his brother's shadow—so he'd acted up, been the anti-George so people had to at least acknowledge him.

Both of them hurting and wanting what they couldn't have.

And now one of them was gone, and still Ryan was being compared to his brother.

And she was facilitating that. Keeping him in George's perfect shadow.

No wonder he'd driven away without looking back.

'Meredith,' she started again, as her mother-in-law busied herself fetching wine glasses and getting the bottle out of the fridge. 'I think we need to talk about George and Ryan. Don't you?'

At her words, Meredith slumped against the fridge door. 'I can't hear it, Gwen. I don't want to know. Can't I keep my memories?'

Her chest hurt. She didn't want to do this. She'd never wanted to do this.

'You can remember George however you want. He was a good man, and a good husband to me for a number of years.' Not all of them, but his mother didn't want to know that. 'But you have another son too. One who is alive, and who wants to be part of your life—who has worked so damn hard to turn his own life around, to be someone you and he can be proud of. If your memories of George are keeping you from loving Ryan... then I don't think that's right. Do you?'

Meredith turned slowly. She looked a decade older, Gwen realised, all in the space of a few seconds.

'You won't tell Evie? I don't want her to grow up hating her father.'

'She won't,' Gwen promised. 'But I won't lie to her either. When she's older, if she has questions, I'll answer them honestly. I'll tell her the great things about him as well as the harder things. Because she'll hear them from other people otherwise. And I want her to know what's true.'

Certainty filled her as she spoke the words. And for the first time since George's accident she knew, without a shadow of a doubt, that she was on the right track. At last.

It was a harder path, she had no doubt. But she didn't want to be Meredith in twenty years' time, still insisting on perfection from someone who could never reach it.

She wanted to live in the real world. Where there was love and trust and support—and where she appreciated it all the more because she knew it wasn't automatic. It was something you worked for.

She wanted that for her daughter too.

And for herself…

'Meredith, I'm going to be spending more time with Ryan. These allegations about

George won't change that. I hope you can find a way to make peace with him.'

'He's the only son I have left,' she whispered. 'I suppose—'

'Mummy!' Evie bounded into the room, fully awake from her nap, and wrapped her little arms around Gwen as she lifted her into her embrace. 'Where's Uncle Ryan?'

'He had to go, sweetie.' Gwen met Meredith's gaze over Evie's head, and she nodded. Finally, some acceptance. A first step, at least. 'But I'll take you to see him again very soon, I promise.'

Just as soon as she'd figured out a way to make everything right again.

CHAPTER ELEVEN

IT HAD BEEN almost two weeks. Practically half a month since he'd seen Gwen, kissed her, held her.

And, God, did he miss her.

As he grabbed his bag and his headphones for the bus ride from the team hotel to the stadium, Ryan tried to put her out of his head, but all he could think about was waking up beside her that first precious morning. Knowing that at last he was where he was meant to be.

Except apparently she didn't agree.

'Hey, Phillips. You got your game head on?' His captain, Alwyn, stopped him halfway to the door.

'Course I have,' Ryan replied automatically.

It was his first game back for Wales, and the coach was taking a huge chance on him just putting him on the bench for it, even for a theoretically friendly warm-up match before the summer tour. He couldn't risk not having his head in the game.

Even if his heart was still with Gwen, in Nantes.

'Good.' Alwyn slapped him on the back and let him continue on his way.

Ryan pulled his headphones over his ears, just like the other lads, blocking out the world and letting him focus on the challenge ahead as he climbed onto the bus.

In just a couple of hours they'd be out there on the field. Well, he'd be on the side-lines, waiting to see if he was needed. But he was in Wales, playing for Wales again. Back where he belonged.

Everything he'd wanted was coming together.

He'd sent his parents his complimentary tickets for the game. Whether they'd come, he had no idea. But he figured he had to try. He had to *keep* trying.

Gwen he had to let work things through on her own. But his parents…maybe there was still hope there. And he wouldn't give up, as long as there was hope.

Preparing for the match happened more or less on autopilot. Ryan went through his usual rituals and routines, as if this were just any other match. By the time it came to run out of the tunnel onto the grass of the stadium, and sing the national anthem, it was too late to worry about the immensity of the situation anyway.

Lining up, he slung his arms around his teammates' waists on either side of him as the band started to play. First, the English national anthem—as the visitors they got to go first. The Welsh male voice choir sang it well, supported by the team and their fans. But it didn't touch Ryan's heart—not really.

But then the first strains of the Welsh anthem 'Land of my Fathers' sounded and Ryan's heart started to beat in time.

'Mae hen wlad fy nhadau yn annwyl i mi...'

The familiar words filled the air as the tune lifted the stadium. The roof was open today, the torrential rain of earlier in the week having cleared at last and the pitch mostly dried out.

'Gwlad beirdd a chantorion, enwogion o fri...'

Ryan lifted his chin, the words coming from memory, learned so long ago. He smiled as he remembered George teaching him the lyrics, before his first proper Wales match as a spectator, so he could sing along. Whatever his brother had done or become in later years, whatever had come between them, they'd been close once. He wouldn't give up that memory either.

'Ei gwrol ryfelwyr, gwladgarwyr tra mad...'

He risked a glance up at the crowds surrounding them. A sea of red shirts and daffodil and dragon hats on one side. On the other, the white shirts and red and white flags of the English supporters. He couldn't make out individual faces at this distance, especially not through face paint and hats and flag waving. But he hoped his parents were up there somewhere.

'Dros ryddid collasant eu gwaed...'

His attention strayed to the men around him—good men, solid teammates, trusted, guys he hoped would become good friends. Not all natural singers, bless them, whatever people said about the Welsh, but they were belting the anthem out all the same.

They were there with him, believing in the same thing. That they could be better than they had been before. That they could keep working to improve. Not just to win— although that definitely mattered too, especially against England. But just to be *better*. To strive towards being the best they could.

'Gwlad, gwlad! Pleidiol wyf i'm gwlad...'

As they hit the refrain, the cry of love for their nation, Ryan looked up at the huge screen at the end of the pitch, the cameras scanning the Welsh crowds as they sang their hearts out.

And then his own words dried up in his mouth as the camera lingered on two particular faces.

'Tra môr yn fur, i'r bur hoff bau...'

Gwen. Gwen and Evie. Both singing along. Evie had a small red dragon painted on her face, and was standing on her seat to sing.

She was here. *They* were here.

And Ryan would have a full eighty minutes—plus half-time and post-game talks—to figure out what that meant.

'O bydded i'r hen iaith barhau.'

The camera swooped away, back to the team, as the anthem came to an end. And then it was time to play, and Ryan had to focus on the game, even from the bench. He forced himself to push Gwen from his mind.

But when Gareth was injured twenty minutes in, with England five points ahead, and Ryan had to run onto the pitch to take his place, all he could think was, *Please let me play well. Play my best, even. For the team. For the coach. For Wales. For me. For Mum and Dad.*

For George's memory.

For Gwen.
And for Evie.

She'd forgotten how nerve-racking it was, having someone she loved out on that pitch, until Ryan came on as an injury replacement in the twenty-first minute. Knowing that every tackle, every hit could break him. That he might come off that field a different man from the one he'd been when he went on.

But she also remembered now the exhilaration and pride. How a whole nation was placing its hopes on his shoulders.

She knew how much it meant to Ryan to be out there today, and her heart was ready to burst with pride for him now he'd achieved it. He'd worked so hard—not just in training, but on becoming the man he wanted to be.

She couldn't wait to tell him how much she loved him for it. And just for being exactly who he was.

But she did have to wait. At least for now.

Joe sat on Evie's other side, explaining the play to her. Gwen listened in with half an ear, but mostly she was just watching. Watching Ryan as he raced up and down the pitch. How intently he focussed on the play. How good his hands were, grabbing the ball out of the air and passing it exactly where it needed to be. How quickly he could be wherever he was needed.

And, yes, how damn good he looked in that Wales kit, with its clinging top and shorts that showed off his thighs...

'Will we see Uncle Ryan now?' Evie asked at half-time.

'Not yet,' Gwen replied. 'After the match is over. There's still another half to go.'

She wanted to, though. She wanted to race down there to the tunnel and through to the changing rooms and find Ryan and tell him everything.

Except, given that Wales were still down at the break, they were probably getting a loudly yelled half-time team talk, firing them up for the second half.

Ryan needed to focus on the game. But that didn't stop her planning out *her* full-time talk in her head.

I'm sorry. She definitely needed to start with that, right? After that, hopefully it would be easy.

Maybe she'd just kiss him. That seemed to solve—and also sometimes cause—a lot of their problems.

The second half kicked off and Wales almost closed the gap within the first five minutes. Gwen found herself sitting closer to the edge of her seat as every second ticked by, clutching Evie's hand tightly enough that she actually asked her to stop.

Gwen couldn't look away from the ball—that white shape blurring through the air from man to man, hands to hands, then flying through space off someone's boot.

Suddenly Ryan was under it, catching it and racing towards the try line, and Gwen stopped breathing altogether.

'Go, Uncle Ryan!' Evie yelled beside her, and she could hear Joe cheering too. But Gwen couldn't cheer. She couldn't do anything but watch as the huge men in white shirts bore down on him, determined to take him to ground.

The crunch of the impact was audible, and a groan of sympathy went up around the stadium. Joe, obviously sensing her distress, reached across and grabbed her hand.

'Look, Mummy, you're on the big screen!' Evie cried.

Gwen couldn't even look. She knew what it would show.

A woman afraid for the man she loved.

The referee had blown the whistle, a penalty in the ruck that had followed the tackle, and the medical team was on the pitch.

'He's sitting up,' Joe said. 'Look, Gwen. He's fine.'

One of the team handed him a water bottle and leaned in to say something. Down on the field, Ryan looked up at the big screen and smiled. Then he raised a hand and waved, and blew a kiss, and Gwen's lungs started working again.

'He's okay,' she whispered. 'He's okay.'

'Are you?' Joe asked, sounding faintly amused now the panic was over.

'I will be.' When she got to talk to him. When she told him she loved him.

When he hopefully said it back.

Just twenty more minutes left on the clock. She could make it through that. Couldn't she?

One last chance.

Less than a minute left on the clock. One last play. When the whistle blew again it would all be over.

Ryan forced himself to focus on the moment, not on Gwen up in the stands. Her face, when he'd been hit in the tackle. The worry—and the love. The hope it gave him.

Wales had a line-out, just ten metres out from the try line. If they could pull this off, get the ball over the line and score one last try, the game would be theirs.

If they couldn't, they'd lose. Simple as that.

Sometimes life came down to two options, and Ryan liked to think he'd got better at picking the right one over the last few years. Making good choices—or at least better ones. But this time it wasn't just up to him.

It was the whole team.

They lined up, the play already agreed, nerves palpable. Across the way, the English team were joking, shouting, trying to break their focus. They wouldn't succeed.

The ball flew, and Dewi caught it. Fast, he passed it back to Ryan, on to Alwyn, and on down the line. Each throw had to go backwards, but with each catch they surged forward, closer and closer. Until the ball came back to him and Ryan instinctively reacted, his feet moving before he even thought, side-stepping, dodging, twisting and then—*yes!*—running, exactly the way his big brother had taught him, so many years ago.

The English defenders were right behind him, but he was too far now, too fast, too determined. He threw himself over the line, grounding the ball with so much force that the grass rucked up behind it—and the whistle blew.

Try.

His first try for Wales in his first game back. It was everything he'd dreamed of.

His teammates raced over to celebrate, to hug him, clap him on the back, insult him in a loving way, the usual.

There was the conversion to follow, of course, but that flew over the posts as an afterthought. The whistle blew and the game was won.

There would be team celebrations for hours. Interviews, showers, pub, the usual.

'Ryan, how did it feel to score the final try?' the TV interviewer asked on the sideline as he was pushed into the frame.

'Uh…amazing.' But Ryan only had one thing on his mind as he scanned the crowds, trying to find Gwen.

'Your first match back too!'

'Yeah, it was pretty special.'

'And there was someone special out in the crowd, watching you today, I understand?'

Ryan looked at her in surprise as she motioned to the big screen. And there, standing at the railings, just metres away from him, he realised, was Gwen, lifting Evie up as she cheered for him.

'Your niece, Evie.'

Ryan grinned. 'Yeah, she's pretty awesome. Her mum's not bad either, actually. Now, if you'll excuse me…?'

Handing the microphone back, he jogged over to where Gwen and Evie waited, Joe behind them. Climbing straight over the railings—to a cheer from the crowd—he picked Evie up, swung her round and kissed her on the cheek.

'You were amazing, Uncle Ryan!'

'You're better,' he told her. 'And I love your dragon.' He pointed to the cuddly red dragon in her arms.

'Taid gave it to me,' she said. 'They're here somewhere too. He said he gave you and Daddy a dragon just like this when you came to your first rugby game. And Nain taught me the words for the anthem too, so I could sing along like you.'

Tears stung his eyes, but he blinked them away.

'They're really trying,' Gwen said. She took Evie from his arms and passed her over to Joe, who knew a hint when he saw one, obviously, as he distracted her by going to look at all the other players swapping shirts and signing autographs further down the pitch.

'I can't believe you came,' he said.

'Of *course* I came. I wasn't going to miss your first game back for Wales. And besides…'

She took a deep breath. 'I needed to tell you I'm sorry. That I love you—who you are now, the person you were always meant to be. And I didn't ever want to push you back into George's shadow, I swear.'

'I'm sorry too,' Ryan said. 'I know how hard this must all be for you. I know how much you loved George, and I respect you wanting to protect Evie.'

'I *did* love George. But I need to move on from our past together. Find a way to forgive him for those awful last few years so I can be happy again. With you, if you'll have me.'

'Always.' Ryan wrapped his hands around her waist to lift her to him, tilting his head to kiss her as another cheer went up all around them. They were probably on the big screen again.

He didn't care.

'You're my future,' he whispered, as he set her down. 'You're everything I've been working towards all this time, even when I didn't know it. You and Evie, and my parents. I want us to have the happy future that you deserve.'

'I want that too,' she murmured back, in between kisses. 'And I know there's still a lot to work out. But… I love you. And it feels like that's a pretty good start.'

'It's the only one I need,' he replied, knowing he'd won so much more than a game of rugby that day.

Then he kissed her again, and knew in his bones that loving Gwen was the best choice he would ever make.

* * * * *

*If you enjoyed this story,
check out these other great reads from
Sophie Pembroke*

Snowbound with the Heir
Pregnant on the Earl's Doorstep
Carrying Her Millionaire's Baby
CEO's Marriage Miracle

All available now!